BETWEEN TONGUES

CONFINGO PUBLISHING

BETWEEN TONGUES

PAUL MCQUADE

First published in the UK in 2021 by Confingo Publishing

249 Burton Road, Didsbury, Manchester M20 2WA

www.confingopublishing.uk

Printed by TJ Books Limited
Art Direction & Cover Design by Zoë McLean

A CIP catalogue record for this book is available from the British Library

ISBN 978-0-9955966-8-9

2 4 6 8 10 9 7 5 3 1

CONTENTS

A Gift of Tongues

His hands swallow mine when he speaks. *Ich liebe dich*. And I can't reply, can't say what I want to say – I am still on Chapter 7: Politics. Unable to respond, I smile. This is how the relationship goes: we muddle along, half understanding. Nods, smiles, and laughter fill the gaps.

The smile has communicated something. He puts a box in my hands. The gold ribbon slips its knot, coils and falls along the table, swimming into the dark below. The red crêpe crackles like dead leaves.

There is a box inside the box. The second made of glass. The light refracts as it emerges, hiding its contents in white light. Only when I cover it with my hands can I see what is inside: a long slab of meat. Pink, glistening.

'*Eine Zunge*,' he says. Chapter 3: Anatomy.

He has bought me a tongue.

It is winter in Berlin. The sun, cloud-veiled, only deepens the city's shadows. The shadows press up against the buildings, the strange music of the city pours along the streets. Sigh of bus doors, percussion of the U-Bahn. People walk, not hearing, but feeling its movement. Couples crowd the bridges of the Spree, lip-to-ear, whispering secrets the river shelters in its long exhale.

Thöre tries to strike up conversation on the S-Bahn. It is late afternoon, the cabin filled with people on their way to the Grunewald. I stand on tiptoe and speak into his ear, so that other passengers cannot hear my *kauderwelsch* German. Small hairs glance against my lips; white arms soft as peach fuzz carry my words deep into his skull.

Kauderwelsch. Gibberish. Gobbledygook.

My German is comprised of Thöre, a textbook, and the lessons that my work makes the new transplants take. Once a week, for an hour and a half and full pay, we sit in a meeting room and talk. Situational German. Please-and-thank-you's. Polite conversation for business lunches. *We look forward to working with you.* No one takes it seriously. Sometimes when we go out, the other new-starts speak entirely in English, even when ordering, not bothering with so much as a cursory *danke* or *bitte*. There is something exciting about this. Something rebellious. I expect someone to snap, to swear, to tell them to speak German, the way I had seen the French do in Paris. I hold my breath and wait.

No one says a thing.

I met Thöre on one such outing. The new staff, two managers, one of the company lawyers. A bar in the east, street level, light spilling out over Soviet high-rises. We sat in our corner with Bavarian wheat beers, suspended safely in a cloud of English. It was the lawyer who disturbed our seclusion, standing up to shout in German across the bar. A man came over. They hugged, kissed – once on each cheek – and he joined us, taking a seat between the lawyer and me. A couple of half-hearted waves and quiet hellos from my compatriots, and the conversation closed over his entrance. The man and the lawyer turned to each other to talk amongst themselves.

When the lawyer popped to the bathroom, the man leaned across and asked if I spoke German. His breath felt alive against my cheek, and under the reek of bar bodies, he smelled of sea salt and coriander. Emboldened by the *Weissbier*, I tried to remember all those meeting-room conversations. The beer made things smoother. I tried to introduce myself.

'You speak *Kauderwelsch*,' he said, in English. 'But it's cute.'

The lawyer returned and they went back to talking in German, though the man – Thöre, he said his name was, *Thöre as in Thor* – looked at me while the woman talked in his ear, smiling a deep, knowing smile.

When I stepped through the door of my apartment later that night, I pulled out the miniature German-to-English dictionary a friend had bought me as a goodbye present, and looked up what Thöre had said to me.

Kauderwelsch. Noun, neuter.

When I forget the word I want, when a phrase is beyond me, coiled slyly on the tip of my tongue, close as the tail end of a dream, *Kauderwelsch* is there, waiting in the space where the other words should be.

The train comes to a stop. Thöre leans down.

'We're here,' he says, his mouth covering, for a moment, the entirety of my ear.

He takes my hand and leads me out into the forest of the Grunewald.

'It is a very simple operation,' the doctor explains in English. 'You don't even have to be put under full anaesthetic. In fact, the results are far better if the procedure is performed in twilight sleep.'

I hold the boxed tongue in my lap. It seems drier now, under the clinic lights. Smaller. Frightened. I wonder if this is a sign that it is sick, like a dog's nose.

'And afterwards, I'll be able to speak German?' I ask.

'Faultlessly.'

Thöre takes my hand in his.

The doctor lists side-effects, reiterating after each how safe the operation is, how unlikely it is that I will suffer anything other than the pure joy of bypassing years of study.

'Strange things, tongues,' the doctor says. 'I have to say, it's really quite a wonderful gift your boyfriend has bought you. Your new tongue will open doors.'

'What about my old tongue?' I ask.

'Don't worry about that,' he replies. 'We take care of everything.'

Thöre squeezes my hand and looks into my eyes. He mouths the words: *Ich liebe dich*. Still unsure what to say, I nod.

'Excellent,' the doctor says. 'A nurse will be along in a moment to get you prepped. Just sign here.'

The pen makes a scratching sound, like an animal trying to escape.

'I can't wait,' Thöre tells me while we wait for the nurse. 'I'm finally going to be able to talk to you.'

'We talk all the time,' I say.

'You know what I mean.'

'I don't,' I insist.

'You will,' he replies.

The first present Thöre bought me was a flat white, the second a textbook. We met at a cafe near my work. The conversation a series of starts and stops. Almost not quites. When he talked for anything longer than a sentence, slowing down to make sure I could make him out, I let the words pass over me like water. I examined the curve of his jaw, how the stubble didn't quite reach his cheeks, the way the sunlight through the window made one eye wolf-yellow. When he asked me about myself, I responded as best I could. I knew the questions from class, but couldn't remember the right answers, only what other people had said. I told him I had a brother when I have two. That one brother is older when I am the oldest. That I am eight-and-twenty instead of twenty-eight. He smiled at each mistake, chin in hand.

'I bought you something,' he said

He slid an oblong of brown paper along the tabletop. I wanted to tell him that he shouldn't have, that it was nice of him, that I would repay the favour by buying him a drink. But I didn't know how. Instead I unwrapped the package, dumbly.

Inside was a textbook. A Japanese woman laughed with a blond man on the front cover. Above them, in slender green font, was written: *Die Gabe der Zungen*.

'Thank you,' I said

I flicked through the pages and saw a phrase.

'The next round is on me.'

Thöre laughed. After coffee, we took the underground in the same direction, Thöre getting off a few stops before mine. He kissed me and told me he would see me soon. After he left, I caught eyes with a woman sitting nearby. She smiled and said: *Sie sind so ein süßes Paar*. I smiled in response, unsure of what she had said. She returned the gesture and returned to her paperback. The exchange pleased me: as if I were just another German on the subway, kissing my boyfriend goodbye. It felt good.

It felt as if I were invisible.

The new tongue is stapled to the inside of my mouth. Dissolvable double-hinges, the doctor explains. Due to the need for movement, it would be impossible to bind the muscles with sutures. Instead delicate little hinges have been affixed to the join between the old flesh and the new. They glitter in the clinic lights as I move a pink hand-mirror in front of my mouth, watching my tongue lick the white walls of my teeth, brush the inside of my mouth. The mirror makes my teeth seem small, but to my tongue, these things are gargantuan: my teeth are cliff-faces, the roof of my mouth a universe wide. I put the mirror down. I shut my mouth. It feels as if I have closed my eyes.

I notice a taste. Slightly salty, like cured bacon, with a faint hint of bergamot. Tea-smoked meat. I use the new tongue to explore further; the hinges butterfly and pull at their fleshy moorings. The taste comes from all over. A taste my old tongue had forgotten. The taste of my own mouth.

'It will take some time to adjust,' the doctor says as I sign my discharge. 'Little things might take you by surprise. Just be prepared.'

'Don't worry, doctor,' I say. 'I'm already getting used to it. The only thing is the hinges. How long will they be there for?'

'A couple of weeks,' he says. 'But we'll get you in for a check-up after that, just to make sure everything's fine and the hinges have fully dissolved.'

'And my old tongue?'

'Don't worry. We've taken care of it. All you have to do now is focus on resting up and enjoying your new life.'

The tongue has made everything new. Even the air. I

feel it pour over the lump of muscle in my mouth, feel it fill each delicate branch of my lungs. It is scented with the green of the Grunewald as we walk out of the clinic, and on the S-Bahn home, the stale coffee on Thöre's breath and the coriander punch of his cologne. Thöre is remarkably quiet. He sits next to me, grinning.

'What?' I ask.

'Nothing,' he says, beaming ear to ear.

'Tell me.'

'It's your accent,' he says. 'Your new one, I mean. You sound like you were born and bred in Hamburg.'

'Don't be ridiculous,' I tell him. 'Why would I speak English with a German accent?'

He laughs. His eyes reflect the trees as they pass by in the window. For a moment a house with a red roof shines there also. His expression is the same as when I make a mistake in German. Amused, affectionate. But I hadn't made a mistake. Had I?

Thöre's Berlin was different to the one I knew. The Berlin in my head, marked only by bars, restaurants, and coffee shops around my work and flat, branched out, connecting, like tendons, the smaller satellites where we met. I knew the city after a month. Not by direction, but by the memories Thöre and I made: seafood in Charlottenburg, slow walks in Mitte, parties in Neukölln with Thöre's friends. They spoke to me in German, first, then switched to English. It seemed as though everyone in Berlin spoke English, to one extent or another. Only Thöre spoke to me in German.

One night in his apartment in Kreuzberg, as I leafed through *Die Gabe der Zungen* in bed and waited for him to finish brushing his teeth, I called through to the bathroom to ask him why, when everyone else spoke to me in English, only he insisted on German. I heard him spit, heard a tap running. He came and stood in the doorway, the band of his underwear folded over slightly where he had put it back haphazardly. He looked at me as if gauging something. The answer he gave was not textbook: he stopped and started, adjusted what he wanted to say, repositioned sentences mid-flow, so that in the end all I was left with were fragments, clauses out of order.

He does not speak to me in English because he wants me to know something. Something about the truth. Or something real. Him. Something real about him. Himself, maybe. The real him.

He climbed on to the bed, moved up my legs with predatory grace, and closed the textbook in my hands as he gave me a mint-sweet kiss. Then he turned out the light. He fell asleep in seconds. I found it harder. The feeling that I had to be alert, in case I missed something, was hard to shake, even though Thöre was no longer speaking. It was impossible to relax. To help me get to sleep, I ran through the vocabulary list I had just been reading.

Augen, Nase, Herz, und Zehen. Eyes, nose, heart, and toes. *Arm* for arm, *Fuß* for foot. And *Zunge* – tongue. Chapter 3: Anatomy. *Die Anatomie.*

This is how I fell asleep: Thöre's mouth to my ear, his sleep-heavy breath keeping time. While I counted tongues, and waited to dream.

I talk to people in shops, on the train, strike up conversations with strangers at work. So excited am I by my newfound ability to speak and be understood. It feels like diving: deeper and deeper into Berlin, with no need to rise and fill my lungs with English. My new tongue has gills. The half-open wounds of the hinges, now dissolved, breathe the city. Berlin tastes of ash and June and ozone.

People ask me if I am from Hamburg. I tell them that I have never left Berlin. They laugh and ask me why I have a Hamburg accent then, and when I tell them I am not German, they say I must have learned from someone who spoke *Hamburgisch*. But the woman at my office is from Frankfurt, and the only other teacher I had was Thöre.

It never felt as if I were learning German with Thöre. It was as though I were learning a language only Thöre and I spoke. From the beginning he taught me to understand him with hand gestures, repetition, and glacial speech. I spoke a language of errors, parataxis, and diminishing returns.

I knew I had made a mistake when Thöre laughed. It was a particular laughter, almost affectionate. As if my mistakes pleased him, though my pronunciation did not. Everything sounded wrong to him. The words the same but unfamiliar, pressed through the meat grinder of my mouth – I butchered the language, he said.

The only sound I made that pleased him was '*ch*', as in *Ich* for I, as in *I love you. Ich liebe dich*. This he said after a month had passed. I didn't understand. To explain, he placed my hand on his chest. His hands swallowed mine. Something beat, warm and urgent, against my palm. The word came into my head in the rhythm of that beat: *das, Herz, das, Herz*. As if the two could not be separate. As if they needed each other. The first nothing without the second. Meaningless. This is what *Ich liebe dich* meant to me: something added, extraneous, something straining, and significant.

I couldn't tell Thöre this. I lacked the words. Instead I

took his hand and placed it on my chest, let him feel my heart beat its own affirmation: *das, Herz, das, Herz, das, Herz.* Then I remembered something from Chapter 3.

'*Herzen,*' I said. Hearts.

He smiled. Almost as if he understood.

'I'm sorry,' he says.

I drum my fingers on the table. Rain falls against the window, muttering its response. A series of sharp taps, long sprays. Morse code on glass, there where the name of the cafe is written back to front. The words *Der Ausguck* seem almost fluent on their hand-drawn pennant.

I pick up my coffee and take a drink. Nothing. I finished earlier, but keep the cup at my mouth so I won't have to respond. While Thöre explains. How things have changed. Since the tongue.

'It's just that,' he continues. 'We've changed. I don't know.'

I gulp air like a landed fish, pretending there is still coffee in my cup.

'I thought the transplant would have made things easier. But it hasn't. It's nothing like the brochure said,' he says. 'You seem like a different person now.'

I put down the empty cup. Slowly. Attempt to work out what I am going to say. A couple appear at the window and peer in, trying to see through the breath on the glass whether there is anywhere to sit. One of them turns and says something to the other. Their words sound strange, as if the glass has inverted them too.

'If I'm not me any more, then who am I?' I ask.

'I don't know,' Thöre replies.

A bell announces the couple's entrance. They take a seat

at the wall behind Thöre, both of them on the same side of the high table, watching the rain against the window while they talk. When they speak to each other, it is still gibberish to me, glass or no glass. Yet it seems familiar. What language is that?

'I'm sorry,' Thöre says. 'But I don't think we should see each other any more.'

The tongue changed everything but most of all it changed Thöre. It was as if a wall had come down. We emerged from our division, freshly gifted with speech. As if all that had come before were just whispers through brick. But it was not only a matter of language. It was all the little things bound up in it: the sighs, the many meanings of a touch, the warmth in his voice that came and went, like a square of sunlight through a window. The world was gold when it was there. But gradually, it began to turn ashen. He no longer talked to me with his chin in his hands. Now it was hands on table, eyes on fingernails. He looked as if he missed something.

Die Gabe der Zungen did not contain a chapter on relationships. I would never have been able to ask him about it, with my old tongue, would never have been able to have a serious conversation about our feelings. The new tongue had changed all that.

'Is everything all right?' I asked him.

He looked up from his fingernails. He seemed surprised to see me there.

'Of course,' he said. 'Everything's fine. Just tired.'

We said no more about it. But I felt as if I had done something wrong. He no longer laughed when I made mistakes. At first, I thought this was because I no longer made them. But soon I couldn't shake the feeling that all I was capable of was mistakes. And Thöre no longer had any patience for them.

I guess, with my new tongue, I should have known better.

I return to my old life, my old apartment, my old Berlin. But with the new tongue in my head, everything is different.

I know I have been back to my flat. I have had to wash clothes, pick up documents for work, make sure nothing is mouldering in the fridge. But when I move around it now, it feels like trespassing.

I try to reconnect with the other transplants from work, to revive the old friendships I had neglected during my time with Thöre. We go to a bar in the east. It is vaguely familiar, but the memory is dim. We settle at a table in the corner and talk in English. The language hangs in the air around us like haze, making us feel safe and invisible. As if to the Germans around us we were nothing but the faintest of shimmers on the farthest horizon.

The lawyer is there. It is the first time I have seen her since Thöre and I broke up. She is the partner of one of Thöre's friends, Elke. A slight brunette whose family ties to Bavarian aristocracy show through in the imperious way in which she ignores me. When I speak, she does not look at me. The others exchange looks. I wonder if I am saying something offensive, but no one interrupts, so I persevere. As the conversation goes on, and empty glasses crowd the table, one of them finally asks: 'When did you start speaking like that?'

'Like what?'

'Like that. Your English is weird, now. It's like you can't really speak it. And your accent. You don't sound like you any more.'

You seem like a different person now.

'Who do I sound like?'

'You sound like you're from Hamburg,' the lawyer says.

'But I'm not,' I say. 'I'm from...'

I sit there, dumb. The tongue in my head lolls lifeless. I try to remember but the word is not there, only *Kauderwelsch*, burning brand-hot, turning my cheeks crimson.

'I didn't mean to offend you,' the man says.

'Don't worry,' I say. 'It's yesterday's snow.'

I hear it, then. The words sound wrong; the voice is not mine. The table seems to move off into the distance. The room is spinning, or I am. Nothing is solid. I excuse myself, telling them the *Weissbier* has gone to my head, and dive into the night air.

The Soviet high-rises tower above me. Headlights cast long shadows along their faces as I try to find a train station. I walk. Time slips away. I do not recognise these streets; they were not part of me and Thöre. And now I am lost. In this city I thought I knew.

I hold my hand out in the road and a car stops. I climb into the taxi. As it drives to my flat, I look out the window, trying desperately to recognise just one building on the other side of the glass. But nothing looks the same. When the driver stops and asks for the fare, I ask if he's sure we're there.

'Positive,' he tells me as he takes the money. 'Hey, are you from Hamburg? My brother lives there.'

I tell him to keep the change.

I thought I would feel safer back in the apartment, doors locked, curtains drawn. But I still can't shake the feeling that the person who lives there is going to come back, that they will demand that I leave and go back to my own home. But where is that? Where am I from?

Without Thöre, I have nothing to do on the train out to the Grunewald except watch, through the window, as the city recedes. The forest slowly wins back its space. As the train approaches the stop for the clinic, I notice a building in the distance, red-roofed, surrounded by trees in neat rows. It is familiar, somehow, though I am sure I have never been there.

The doctor places my tongue in clamps, the long root of muscle drying in the air, and runs his fingers along the small bumps where the gills of the tongue have closed shut.

'Excellent,' he says. 'Barely a scar. How are you finding it, any problems?'

'No,' I say. 'It seems to be working fine. I speak German, now. No problems.'

'And faultlessly, too, I have to say. Your boyfriend must be pleased. Is he working today?'

'No,' I reply. Then: 'Yes. I mean, yes, he's working, but no, he's not my boyfriend. Not any more.'

'I'm sorry to hear that,' he says. His eyes are wet, glistening with sympathy in the clinic lights. It is strange to see the man that way. He looks like a little boy. And yet, he doesn't seem surprised.

'Does this happen a lot?' I ask.

'It is a danger,' he says. 'But most of the time, no. It depends, you know? On the people. The new tongue helps people speak, that's all. Sometimes it's a blessing, and in other cases...' He shrugs. 'Sometimes, post-transplant, things just fall apart. Your guess is as good as mine why. They just do.'

'Doctor,' I say. I hesitate, not wanting to offend him. I put my hands on my knees and look down at them as I speak. 'I'm sorry, doctor, but I want you to give me my old tongue back.'

He puts his hands over mine.

'I'm sorry,' he says. 'But I can't.'

'But it's mine,' I say. 'It's *my* tongue.'

'When you give up your tongue,' he says, 'you give it up. You can't go back to it. It's a problem of auto-immunity: you can take in a new tongue, if it's managed properly. But your body remembers the old one, and if you try to put it back in, as if it were something new, you would confuse your defences. Your body would try to destroy it.'

'What have you done with it?'

The doctor hesitates.

'I can't really tell you,' he says. 'There are issues of... confidentiality.'

'Doctor,' I say, 'it's my tongue. I don't think you'll be breaking confidentiality if you tell me where it is.'

'That's the thing,' the doctor says. 'It's not your tongue any more.'

'What do you mean?'

'Perhaps...' he says. 'Perhaps it would be better if I showed you.'

We had gone to a restaurant on Charlottenstraße for my birthday. Thöre picked German wines, regional specialities, laid all of Germany out on a table for me. The soft lights of the restaurant made everything gleam and blur.

A taxi back, and we were walking unsteadily up the stairs to Thöre's place, bodies soft and lush with wine. Thöre pressed me against the wall of the stairwell, then pressed a box into my hands, his swallowing mine. Then lip to ear, he whispered: 'One last gift.'

The box was black, its join sealed with a disc of red wax and the imprint of a 'T'. A key wrapped in red crêpe, small bow around its waist, nestled on a mound of grey silk. Next to it lay a strand of snowdrops.

'A key?' I asked. Chapter 2: The Home.

'Aye,' he said. The sound of the word, made strange by his mouth, was almost musical: as if the affirmation were carried away by it, the vowel now a note, fading, *legato*, as Thöre plucked the key from its swaddling and placed it in my hand. Little teeth of metal dug into my palm.

I turned the key in the lock. Thöre stood behind me, his hands on my shoulders, watching, seeing from just above my eye-level, his own home open to me with the swing of a door. I knew what to expect: a minimalist art print in a black frame, a concrete vase with three plastic lilies, dust on their mouths, and a glass sphere for percolating coffee. Yet for some reason, opened with a key that was my own, it seemed different. As if by some sleight of hand the room behind this door had vanished, replaced by another through subterfuge and shifting compartments.

Thöre swept me off my feet. Literally. One arm buckled the hinge of my knees, so that I fell back and into the other. The key in my hand flew up in the air.

It took me over an hour to find it again the next morning. When I locked the door behind me on the way to work, I wondered whether the same apartment would greet me that evening, or if each turn of key would always make things feel new. A new apartment, a new Thöre. A new me.

The doctor punches a code into the wall. His hands are sheathed in latex gloves, powder blue. There is a brief sigh as the door swells open at the press of a hand. They seem so small, in those gloves. Like the hands of a child.

There is darkness before us. Then fluorescent lights

shudder, flicker, race along, until off in the distance, the corridor is nothing but light. The doctor leads me down the corridor, explaining that normally this area is out of bounds, but that he wanted me to understand how it worked. We walk by glass boxes in airtight recesses. In each one, a stub of muscle glistens.

'Where do you get them?' I ask.

'Donations,' he replies. 'Donations. The tongue you have now, for example, was donated by the family of someone who had recently passed. Originally from Hamburg, I believe.'

He stops in front of a case. The tongue inside seems impossibly small. I imagine it must have belonged to some sort of animal.

'This is your tongue,' he says.

I look at it. I look at it the way an animal looks at its reflection, recognising there something strangely familiar and at once completely other. How had I never seen it before, its swell, the lumps at the root, those bumps on its surface, like a secret written in Braille? Is the new tongue like this? Are all tongues the same? Even on the way through this room filled with them, I had only noticed their pinkness, their wetness, how fat they seemed, lying there disused.

'Unfortunately, it already has a buyer. A politician. Tongues like yours fetch a premium,' he says.

'What do you mean like mine?' I ask.

'People whose mother tongue is English,' he says. I am alarmed by the mistake. It feels dangerous. Like a trap about to spring shut.

'But it's not,' I tell him. 'English isn't my mother tongue.'

He is visibly unsettled.

'But that's what your boyfriend wrote on the application form. Mother tongue: English.'

'No,' I say, realising that in the time Thöre and I had been together he had never asked me. 'He was wrong. English isn't my mother tongue.'

'Oh,' he says, crestfallen. 'Do you have any proof?'

'What kind of proof would I have? Look, wouldn't you get in trouble if you sold him my tongue, knowing full well that, proof or not, there's still a danger that it's not worth the "premium".'

He sighs. 'I'll tell him the situation and see what he says. He might still want it. But if not, it's yours for the standard price.'

'Does this mean I can have my tongue back?' I ask.

'Yes and no,' he says cautiously. 'Like I said, we can't put the tongue back in your head. But we can give you it back, I suppose. If the buyer no longer wants it. You'd have to buy it, of course. And take care of it. It has to be kept cool and moist. When people purchase the tongues as gifts, we supply a glass box. Technically there's no reason that it couldn't be kept in one long-term.'

'Please.'

The word hangs in the air for a moment, in that room of quiet tongues. I hear the rawness in it, how desperate I must sound to him. I wonder if the tongues hear it too.

The doctor nods.

We make the necessary arrangements. I fill in paperwork, declaring that I will take responsibility for the tongue, that it will be gifted to Thöre on a date to be confirmed. The doctor signs off on the lie. After the paperwork is filed, I ask him why he is helping me.

'Let us just say that I have a certain amount of sympathy for your situation,' he says. He sticks his tongue out on its side: along its underbelly I see faint arcs, like the closed slits of gills. 'The marriage didn't last long after. Like I said, sometimes things just fall apart.'

The doctor shakes my hand at the entrance. His hand seems bigger to touch, almost gargantuan. Yet it fits perfectly into mine, as if made of a piece. I turn to leave but stop, unable to shake something.

'One thing,' I ask. 'Do you keep the tongues until they find a new owner?'

'We try,' he says. 'But some tongues aren't as popular. We keep them as long as we can, but if we can't find an owner, we have to get rid of them.'

'What do you do with them?'

'Well,' he says. 'You'll have noticed this clinic is in the Grunewald. There's a reason for that. If we can't find a new home for a tongue, they get processed into fertiliser. It's quite interesting, actually: the composition of the tongue, all the things that go into making it, produce a fertiliser that makes things grow almost twice as fast as normal. We sell it to a small paper mill nearby. Maybe you saw it on the way in, it has a red roof?'

'A paper mill?' I ask. An image flashes in my memory of a house with a red roof. It feels as if I had lived there, once.

'Yes,' he says. 'It's owned by a pretty famous publishing company. They make language textbooks. *Die Gabe der Zungen.* Maybe you've heard of them?'

That night in my apartment, I count tongues in my head, but can't sleep. Each time I close my eyes I see them: all the tongues no one wanted, falling between blades, their pink meat turned to slurry, poured on to saplings. The slim frames shake with the weight of the tongues. The leaves are slick with them. From little acorns, mighty oaks. Then with an axe, down they go. Cut and pulped, pressed, printed. And the people carry them with them as they walk, under arms, wrapped in brown paper, just as I had done – the last of someone's tongue.

I get up to fetch a glass of water. The apartment is quiet, still. Peaceful. I am growing used to its space, the hush of the cars below the window. The feeling that someone might come in at any minute has lessened.

I pour ice cubes from the freezer into a glass then fill it from the tap. Stopping for a moment, I go back and take something out of the refrigerator. Seated at the kitchen counter, the clink of the ice fills the quiet space, as I watch my warm fingerprints fade from the chilled surface of a glass box.

It lies there, under glass. My tongue. The one I can't put back in my head. It is strange to have it there, that I should be the one to keep it. It belongs to me, but at the same time, it doesn't. I can't shake the feeling that I am only keeping it safe for a time, that it is something held only until it can be passed over. Like a gift. Is this how Thöre had felt, safe-keeping the tongue that now moves in my head?

A car's headlights drift through the window. Shadows dance along the walls of the apartment. Beyond the glass, Berlin glitters in the night.

He is out there, somewhere. Thöre. I will never see him again. I am sure of it. A wall has lifted itself between us, something not uncommon in this city. Our lives take place on either side of it. Any conversation would happen only through the bricks. Perhaps he has already found someone else. Perhaps he will buy them a tongue; gift it to them in a box of red crêpe, in that apartment where he had once given me a box sealed with a gold ribbon.

I still have a key. I could open that door, step between the walls, and enter. But each turn of the key, something changes. The Thöre in that room is a stranger. I do not speak the language he speaks. Though we share a tongue, now.

Under glass, a long slab of muscle. Pink, glistening. *Eine Zunge*. A gift, kept for the time being. One day, I will give it to someone. I will say the words: *Ich liebe dich*. And they will not know what to say. But, perhaps, they will respond. Somehow. In another language. One of slightest touches, of tender embraces – of hands, and lips, and tongues. One day. *Eines Tages*.

An Inheritance

The cabin appears then disappears. As we wind up the mountain road, the radio loses its signal – crackles, flares. There is a voice behind the sounds but the words break apart. The cabin reappears, disappears, the road snakes left and right and the car drives upward. Gravity pushes everything backward: my lungs into my spine, the seatbelt into my chest, the rubber ball on the dashboard into the swell of the grey plastic.

Then we are there. The cabin on our left, not much, after all that. But to the right, the world drops away. The valley stretches out infinite white. The city below is lost behind the thin waists of the pines and the burden of snow on their long shoulders. Some shiver and bare their deep green needles.

'Let's get inside,' Dean says. 'It's freezing out here.'

The car heater has begun to ping cool. A ghost of chill air is creeping into the car. But I want to stay, safe inside, looking out over the valley. The snow itself is strange to me; not a California product, not something I ever grew up with.

Every time I scrunch a ball of it in my hands and it becomes solid it is a tiny miracle.

But we did not come here for snow.

'OK,' I say. 'I'll get the boxes. You go inside and get the heating on.'

Dean grunts. He trudges through the snow to the old door and vanishes.

*

When had he last bought clothes?

He thinks he might have bought a shirt two years ago, in Wisconsin, but he can't be too sure; it could have come from a friend of his there, Fred, when he left the work to get married. Had that been this shirt? What colour had it been?

He is realising that at the age of thirty-two, he might never have bought himself a shirt. A man without his own shirt. That wouldn't do.

He stops outside a shop in town, the thick bundle of an overcoat under his arm. A good solid coat. It would last. That was what he had come for. But he has some money left and he won't go back to his house without a shirt to his name. As he looks at the shirts in the window display, he realises they are all button-downs, brightly coloured things, some in silk.

Someone whispers in his ear.

He drops the coat as he turns. There is no one on the street.

He picks the coat up and puts it under his arm. Shaken, but he is resolved. He wanders around town looking for a shirt. At every shop, he hears a whisper, thinks he sees someone out of the corner of his eye.

He finds one, thick flannel, red and black tartan.

The red calms him. It reminds him of blood: of things pulsing under the surface of his skin, of life under this endless blanket of snow, of spring.

When he goes up to pay, the girl at the register asks him if he's new in town.

'Just bought a place up the ridge,' he says. 'Working at the mill.'

'Up on the mountain?' she asks. 'Must get cold. You should come down here more often. Get a drink down at the bar on the corner, they do good food too. Nice place to take a girl out.'

The last she says without looking at him: her eyes are on the shirt, red and black, folding over. She wraps it in thin paper and places it gently in a paper bag. There is something about the softness of it; the crinkle of the onion-skin wrapping, the way the brown paper feels as if he could tear it with a touch. He tries to respond but all he can think of is tearing up paper. He realises he has yet to say anything; he is standing in front of her, dumb, as she holds out the paper bag. His cheeks burn. She laughs.

'I'm Rose,' she says.

'Jack,' he replies. He likes the red in her name.

*

The cabin is surprisingly well-furnished inside, if furnished is what you could really call it; it seems more bric-a-brac, leftovers, things of no importance and no taste. A copper coffee pot with a serpentine spout sits on the open range, left to watch over the seating area from its vantage in the kitchenette. None of the seat cushions match. On the small coffee table in front of the sofas, an ashtray harbours fag-ends above the gold impression of a seven-pointed star.

There is a photo frame by the door. Dean and a young woman stand next to a mint-green Chevrolet pick-up, his arm around her waist, cinched in by a pale pink belt. No, not Dean. The same jawline, the same thick sideburns, but the nose is too thick; there are knots in the bone from where it has clearly been broken more than once.

'You look just like your grandfather,' I call out.

'What?' Dean pokes his head out of the doorway across from the sofas. An oil painting of a lake hangs next to the doorway, slightly askew. The image and Dean take turns being out of balance.

'This,' I say, holding the photo frame up. 'It's your grand-father, right? You look just like him.'

Dean comes and takes the photo from my hands.

'Jesus,' he says. 'That's an old one. That must be Grandma Rose next to him. Bit of a looker back in the day, wasn't she?'

'We should take it back with us.'

'Why?'

'Wouldn't your granddad like to see it?'

Dean doesn't answer. He looks at the photograph, seeing something there I cannot.

'I'm not sure he would see it even if we brought it back for him,' he says. 'But we'll take it. It's good to see him like this.'

'He looks happy,' I say.

'I hope so.'

Dean cocks his ear as if listening to someone speak, something he does whenever he is thinking. His eyes stare through the picture. I try and listen for what he must be hearing, but only the sound of leaves fills the house, the to and fro crunch of them, like the slow rock of surf.

*

He pulls on his red and black shirt and rises. The dark in the corner scuttles back into itself and hides, balled, like a cat. The morning light keeps it at bay. He is grateful for that. But still, he thinks he hears it talk: little words just out of earshot.

He arches his back and hears something crack. He will have to get a new mattress if he's ever going to bring Rose back.

Rose.

The name keeps him warm as he moves into the other room, still bare, but with one new addition: a copper coffee pot he had bought with Rose at the second-hand shop on Main. She said it put her in mind of the Arabian nights. He had liked the soft rise of its spout: a gentle S that reminded him of the necks of the swans he used to feed with his mother when he was small.

He makes coffee, butters some toast, and sits on the floor to breakfast. The dark in the corners of the room watches him eagerly, whispers its not-quite-words. But he pays it no mind.

Rose.

The apartment is too bare for her. She has hinted at coming up, especially this last month, but he is too embarrassed by what he lacks, by this spartan life he leads in the woods. He wants to show her something else, a whole panoply of little things that might speak to her of fullness. Something more than the stark Oregon winter and the harsh men who work it, out here in the woods.

He has been setting aside his wages at the mill. A ball of notes and coins under his mattress. The swell of it presses into his back when he sleeps, sometimes rousing him to that thin surface between dream and waking, where he is sure he can hear someone speaking.

He had planned to keep the money for security. To know that he had it to rely on; it had never occurred to him that he might want to spend it, that he might want to burn it up, all this money that he had never had before – transform it into something with more value.

He looks at the copper pot. He likes that it reminds him of Rose, and his mother, and the graceful necks of swans. It is much more than itself. It has an underwriting to it, a separate part, beyond the copper and the spout, the purpose and the utility.

He washes his face and dabs it dry with a towel.

The door has not frozen shut that day. He takes it as a good sign. He looks at the cabin's insides before he goes to work and imagines what it might look like, filled with this writing of life and small objects.

*

'What do you want to do with the coffee pot?'

'Throw it in the trash,' Dean says. 'Or in the charity box if you think anyone will buy it.'

It seems a waste to throw it away, but when I pick it up, I can see the bottom is rusted through. Strange that it had been kept out in the open like that, unusable as it was. Dean's granddad probably just liked the look of the thing.

We pack up boxes for the tip, boxes for the charity shop, boxes for Dean's parents, boxes for ourselves. Most of it is junk. And yet it feels like such a waste, to throw it all away, without knowing where it came from.

'I wish your granddad could be here to help us with this,' I say. 'I feel like I'm throwing away things he might care about.'

'You're a classic hoarder,' Dean says from the other room. 'It's all junk. We're meant to clear it out so we can sell it, not take half the crap home with us. Besides, if my granddad could be here, we wouldn't have to be selling the place.'

'I know,' I say. 'But still.'

Dean comes through from the other room in a red and black checked shirt.

'What do you think?' he asks. 'It's what he was wearing in the picture you found. Hanging up in the closet, still fine. There's something stuck to the sleeve, though. I think it's pine resin.'

Dean scratches at a patch of stickiness on the sleeve. The substance flakes to white, but will not budge. It drags the fibres of the shirt into it, twists and turns as a solid disc, but will not tear, will not pry off. It is so caked in it seems obvious that it has withstood several washings. A part of me admires it its stubborn devotion.

'Handsome,' I say. 'You should take it. It suits you.'

'Maybe I will,' he says. 'Some good's got to come of this.'

'It's all good.'

'How d'you figure that?'

'Well, the doctors say your granddad's been sick for a while, right? So it's good he's finally being treated. I can't imagine what it must have been like for him back then. No doctors. Just a bunch of people cutting into brains. I mean, he's in a nice facility, being treated, has his own room. He's not having pieces of his brain removed.'

'Maybe it would have been better if he had,' Dean says. 'Or maybe it would have been better if no one found out. He lived fine before. I don't get why it's been so much worse since.'

'Maybe you just didn't know it was as bad as it was,' I say. 'But it seems like they were happy. Maybe that's what we should focus on. The fact that they were happy. Despite it all.'

'I guess you're right,' he says, then half smiles. 'Despite it all.'

He smoothes down the sleeves of the shirt, presses its folds into himself, wraps his arms around his waist to bring it tight, and smiles. For a moment, it is as if all that has happened has left his face: he seems younger, fresher, uncreased. He seems like a different man.

'It suits you,' I say. 'You should keep it.'

'Yeah,' he says. 'Maybe we should keep some things.'

*

He gathers enough to bring her there. Enough to feel as though he is not insulting her with sparseness, though it will always be less than she deserves. He has things he never dreamed of: cushions, a sofa, dish towels, mint soap. Every time he sees her he wears the shirt he bought the day he met her.

'You need to wash that shirt,' she says.

'Oh really?' he asks, wrapping his arms around her.

'Well, there's sap stuck to the sleeve. But just make sure it smells the same.'

'What does it smell like?'

'You,' she says.

They stand there for a moment, in the space between the

kitchenette and the seating area, in front of the bedroom door. Beyond the windows the sun begins its descent down on the other side of the mountain. And the dark begins to speak. It has never spoken while anyone else is there. It is growing bolder now.

He sways with Rose in his arms. She begins to hum. The sound passes through her ribs and into his, in his lungs, up his spine. And the words in the dark seem to tremble and scatter. Like smoke blown in the wind. He heaves a sigh.

Rose's song is in his throat. He feels better.

The sound rolls over the copper coffee pot, the sofa cushions, out the window. The words melt into air.

*

'What was your grandma like?'

'Lovely,' he says. 'Sweet as pie. Real Midwest. Viking ancestry, all that stuff.'

'But I mean,' I begin. 'But I mean. What was she *like*?'

'What do you mean?'

I gesture with my left hand to the box of old things, as if they could communicate what I can't, as if the clown figurine could explain what kind of person she was, what she had dreamt of, what it had been like, with a husband like that.

'Did it ever show?' I ask.

'What, that Grandpa was crazy?'

'Mentally ill,' I say. He rolls his eyes.

'Not that I could tell. She seemed happy. Happiest one in the family, every Christmas, every birthday, always smiling. I don't think she had some sort of double life or anything.'

The red and black shirt moves awkwardly on him, all its creases at odd angles, as if conjuring the ghost of another body. He sifts through the last of the debris: a couple of records, a spinning top, a brass button marked with a ship. The rest of the house is empty. Even the corners are pristine, swept clean with a navy dustpan set whose brush handle hung snapped in two. Dean had to grip the thing near the base to really get into the corners. The imprint remains, below the nail of his index, a small red crescent. Like the arc of a blood moon.

He is so fixed on emptying out the house; his eyes have a faraway look, and sometimes he tilts his head to the side, as if listening to instructions.

'How often did you come here?'

'Not that much,' he says. 'It's a bit far. The coast is better in the summer and there are too many trees for skiing. Not a lot to do here. But Grandpa kept telling me about it when I was a kid, saying he would take me up here, show me it, how great it was. The way he went on, I thought it would be a bit more than this.'

He has a point: it isn't much. And yet, it seems too much. All these things in boxes, some for keeping, some for charity. And no way of telling what they meant. It is as though someone had taken the letters of the alphabet and scattered them about the cabin, and neither Dean or me knew how to put them back together in a way that would mean anything. A love letter in a foreign language.

Someone had loved it once.

*

The dark ebbs and flows. Something like a lunar pull brings it out. When he is alone it whispers to him. Sweet, sickly things. Like the slow spill of molasses.

But when she hums it is all gold light.

There is money under the mattress again. He has stopped buying things; the cabin is full of their life, now, a history of bric-a-brac, the clown figurine so ugly she had just had to have it, the button they had found on a bar top. She had told him a story about its previous owner: a sailor who had torn it off toying with it, thinking of a lost love in some far off land – *Karamesh*, she had said. He had laughed, but hadn't corrected her. It wasn't until years later she learned that the city's name was Marrakesh. But it didn't matter. She had rewritten it for both of them. One day, they were going to go to Marrakesh. After.

But for now he has to save up for the ring.

When he thinks of the future, he sees himself in this cabin, showing his children what it all meant, how they had met, how she had changed everything.

Rose is doing the dishes and humming. She smells of lavender, soap suds, and the clean fresh scent of her perspiration. When he wraps his arms around her, she leans her head into the cusp of his neck.

'You need to get a new shirt,' she says. 'You've had that one forever. And there's stuff stuck to the sleeve.'

He smiles. The conversation is well practised; she knows he will not give it up, he knows she knows. But they talk, like this. And she hums against his chest. And the dark grows quiet.

*

It is strange to go through his grandparents' things. Every moment, he feels as though he is about to come across something he shouldn't, as if, in this tiny little cabin on the edge of the Oregon woods, there is another history, a part of his family that, once he has read it, will change the one he has for ever. Adoption papers. A bigamous marriage licence. DNA results that prove his father is not his father. Or worse still, a stale prophylactic, an antique marital aid, vintage pornography.

He had never realised how tenuous his image of his grandparents was. Or that he had never really known them. The people they were, at least. Grandma and Grandpa, yes. But this, this cabin, all these things. It is as if he has found a letter in a bottle. But in a foreign language. Like Chinese script. A jumble of shapes and objects arranged just so. But he knows nothing of the arrangement, or what they might mean.

Every question Sam asks is a jolt. Stops him thinking. But he is glad for the company, and the distraction. There is another sound in the cabin he can't quite put his finger on: a voice at the edge of hearing, whispering something urgent, but when he strains to hear it there is only the wind rolling down the mountain.

He cocks his head to the side and tries to hear the mountain speak.

*

What will our children keep?

Not that we have much: we share a one-bedroom in the city with a few pieces of tat, some reclaimed furniture. Not ours, originally. But they are more ours than anything new could be: we have written our lives on them. Food poisoning from the Chinese round the corner, by the European import store, the *Marktplatz*. When we had lain on the couch all day, beaded with sweat, clutching each other and watching daytime TV. A chef had gutted a catfish and Dean had run to the bathroom to be sick. The memory is pressed, like a thumb in wax, on the bare surface of the sofa we picked from a skip. And the sofa remembers it.

Looking through his grandparents' things, I feel comforted that we are taking some. Even if we don't remember them. The things do. The things remember us. Even if our children don't, even if their children don't: the sofa remembers, the photos remember. If only we could speak the language of things.

*

Rose knows something is off, that her husband is becoming a little unhinged. But when she holds him in her arms, it feels as if he is solid once more.

She has heard of people who are sick in the mind. And he is not one of them.

So she puts it down to eccentricity. And they go on living, gathering little things, little pieces of life. And they marry, save up, have children, expend themselves in the making of their children's lives. The years go by. She is happy.

Sometimes, when she looks back, she can hardly believe all the time that has gathered behind her, like one long shadow.

The doctor tells her there is a shadow on her breast.

When she thinks of life, she feels blessed to have had so much.

And yet, when the doctor talks, all she can think is that she has not had enough, that she has yet to see her grandson marry, that she has yet to go to Marrakesh.

And she worries most about what will happen to her

husband.

The doctor talks. There is an image of her that is not her: black and white, ghostly shapes. And that shadow.

It means something. It would like to speak to her, but she cannot hear it. There is only the numbness of the voice.

He asks her: 'Rose, do you understand what I've told you?'

'Yes,' she says. 'I am going to die.'

And all she can think of is what she will leave behind.

*

There are boxes for the charity shop, boxes for his parents, boxes for the tip.

The cabin is gutted, spotless. It is ready for new life.

The new owners won't remember the life that came before them, unless they find, somewhere we have missed, a button with a ship, a photograph slipped between the wall and the foundation. Something little, left only to signal that the life there has left.

But when I think of the things in the charity box, recycling, moving round again, reused, remembering, it makes me smile.

The sun has set when we pack up the car. A dark night has settled over the mountain, pierced here and there by starlight. The dark all the darker for it. I can't imagine how they had lived here, in the woods just out of town, with all this dark around them.

Dean drives us back to town with one hand on the wheel, the other scratching at the hard patch of red and black on the sleeve of his grandfather's shirt.

I imagine our son finding that shirt in an old box, rooting

through our things after our deaths. He and his girlfriend prying at the sap-stain as if trying to pick off a scab, talking about what it could be, joking, luridly, about bodily fluids, because it all comes down to the body in the end. A finger on the arc of an ear. An ear to an invisible voice. A shirt, a body, a life.

What will it mean? For us. For them.

Dean tilts his head to the side, as if he can hear the answer.

This Impossible Flesh

The hardest part is the eyes. Their removal requires precise and controlled skill. My husband is the surgeon. My fingers do not move so measuredly. Above the flesh they tremble. Till must guide me through the layers of fat and muscle that enshrine the eye in its orbital socket. It is the only operation he cannot perform himself.

Our son lies on the slab. He has my left leg, my husband's right. No arms. Not yet. Till and I need them until our son is complete. Despite this, he is beautiful. As Till places his own eye in our son's face the patchwork skin settles tight around it, drawing his features into relief. Eyes, nose, and jaw in golden mean. The perfect son, even before life. This is what we made him.

The organs and muscular system were endlessly complex. Slivers of our flesh placed in jars and left to grow in chemicals fragrant with alcohol and foxglove. The heart had a sentimentality to it, but it was the lungs that left the strongest impression: pale pink branches of alveoli blossoming in their translucent casings.

The organs were something of the two of us. As a child

should be, though for us that was not entirely possible. Perhaps this is why I liked the organs most. The difference was not so apparent in flesh. In the bones you could see it: Till's were whiter, more calcified from the years he had spent growing up in Fuchsberg near the Austrian border. Fresh milk every morning and walks in the country air were not something my family could afford in Frankfurt. My bones were more porous, yellowed. The sickliness of cities lay in them. The difference was still there, the join visible despite Till's fusing of the two as he made our son's skeleton.

Till wanted children. He had been an only child in this house on the hill, which bears the name Fuchsstein like a curse, and casts its shadow over the town of Fuchsberg below. His father, the town doctor, had built it for his mother; for the many children she had wanted but never had. Something had gone wrong with Till's delivery: tubes had twisted, things had come unstuck in the womb. She died in labour and his father died with her. All the fire of the man extinguished as his wife gave in to ethered black. Till wanted something different. He wanted life to come to Fuchsstein.

He had been a gaunt thing when I met him, barely there – a spectre haunting nothing more than himself, surprised to be at medical school in Frankfurt, surrounded by so many people. Yet for all that, the city was lonely for him. It seemed to hold as little life as Fuchsstein, only more bodies. He had been so unsure of himself then, when I met him in a cafe on Berliner Straße, near the gallery where he had gone for the first time to see art. He had an accent, couldn't quite say 'Kunst' the way we did in Frankfurt. I taught him, over sour coffee in his student flat, the words from my mouth to his, longer the more confident he grew: *Kunst, Kunstgriff, künstlich.* Art, artifice. Artificial.

We settled in Fuchsberg when Till graduated. Frankfurt held nothing for me. It never had. I had no love of Meier's art gallery, the cruel spires of the cathedral, the ashen days that drown, eventually, in the river Main. I had found in Till something larger than Frankfurt, something more vital. We didn't need the city. We had each other, and a place to call home, and that was all we needed. Then.

Fuchsstein brought a change in Till. Perhaps my presence there, or simply the shock of being back in the big house with its sad rooms, all finished with delicate touches: handmade dolls of fine bone china, rocking horses saddled in gold leaf. None ever used. Till wandered those rooms at night. I could hear him through the walls, the shift of his footsteps on the dark oak, the way each stone of the house adjusted to his movements, sighed slightly.

I found him one night on the landing of the second floor, hand on the door jamb of the rocking horse room, moonlight streaming through the windows. He seemed thinner, there, shirt unbuttoned, pale skin goosefleshed. His long limbs moved slowly as he turned to me. The shadow on the wall was larger than him. The chalk-light caught a trace of liquid near his eyes.

'It's unfair,' he said.

'What?'

'That we can't,' he said. 'Can't have children.'

Something swelled in my chest.

'Come to bed, love,' I said. 'You're a doctor. You of all people should understand these things.'

He looked surprised, as if I had reminded him of something.

'I'm going to go read,' he said, a faint tremor in his voice. He sounded almost excited.

He read. For weeks after. And when he wasn't reading, he was talking feverishly about things I couldn't understand. Something about Erasmus Darwin and what needed to be done. Workmen came to renovate the basement, hauled in medical equipment and electric generators.

'A precaution,' Till told them. 'You never know what a storm can do.'

When Till revealed his plan to me, he held my arms in his hands and pressed his face against mine, as if to keep me still. The words flowed over me. His eyes filled my vision. That close it seemed as if I could see inside them – see the part of him that made him him. His eyes were the colour of cut cucumbers. The colour was all I could see.

Till had always wanted to have children. I had never wanted to because I couldn't. It was a medical fact. An impossibility of flesh. In Frankfurt, when this was becoming clear to me, I had been overcome by the sheer weight of that realisation. I told myself I had never wanted it in the first place. You learn to forget, the pain, the loss that comes with the decision to live through. The letting go in order to rise. But in me still the seed of it lingered. And as Till spoke, the thinnest part of hope began to stir.

Hope will take you further than you think. It will make things succumb to a sinister logic. There will be no part of yourself you will not sacrifice. A leg, an eye, a thin sail of skin. It will bring you past the edge of going back, will bring you to a basement dark, your son on a slab and your husband with a scalpel. You will have no fear. I have no fear. Now that my son's eyes are in place, now that Till is ready for the final surgery, half of me seems too little to pay.

'Is it time?' I ask Till as he steps away from our son. Armless, the torso ends in abrupt bluntness, but so peaceful is his face, so perfect its balance of Till and myself that it is easy to forget. Till wraps his arms around me in answer. This is the last time it will be possible. He looks at me with one green eye and in it I see my own blue reflected. I bow my head. Till prepares to remove our arms, attaching first mine, then his own with my assistance. We have given all we can, given what we must for life to spring from us – we men of paltry flesh and unshakeable desire.

And still something is missing. The one thing we cannot pass down. The flesh, yes, and the land. This house with its ailing windows where the breath gathers at night. These shall pass from our hands to his, as so much has passed from us to him, but the soul – the soul is irreproducible, cannot be partitioned, divided or shared. And so, on this chill night in Fuchsberg, my husband and I do what we can to give him life, substituting in place of the soul the great cobalt roar of lightning.

The generators thrum. Electricity travels up long rods to the roof. Till puts his remaining hand in my own. This is the most difficult part. The wait. All parents experience it; this feeling like an indrawn breath. This time before the world is made new. I am almost too weak to stand it, and Till seems to share this fatigue, slumping on my shoulder where the arm is still attached.

'I hope there's enough of us left,' he says. 'To look after him. To raise him the way a boy should be raised.'

'He'll never be a normal boy,' I say, resting my head on top of Till's hair. 'But as long as there is enough left of us, for him and for us, then I'm happy.'

'Life,' he says, 'is an odd thing.'

The storm comes. Slowly, then suddenly. The wind rises to a shriek. Lightning strikes the generator rods. Blue arcs surge along wires to the slab, down into clips attached to nerve endings and muscle groups. First the fingers twitch on the hand that had been Till's, then on the one that had been mine. Our son's arms try to rise, unstopper bags of blood: three pints mine, three pints Till's. The blood courses black through clear tubing; dives into the intricate network of veins. The heart – part mine, part his – begins to beat. Fiercely, loud enough to shake the house to its foundations. The lungs draw their first breath.

We have sacrificed so much. But there will be enough left. There must.

Our son opens his eyes: one green, one blue. And he is beautiful.

Les Archives du Cœur

The bike wheels skit and bounce on the loose dirt path. The smell of hot rubber and the smell of the sea: waves, to the left, and the final site coming into view from behind its fan of magnolia, cypress, and Japanese spruce. Completely unassuming, the final building on the tour through Teshima is nothing but dark wood and a plain, low roof. Compared with the gossamer space on the hillside, the pored concrete and soft wind of the Nishizawa and Naito museum, this last building could be mistaken for an office. But the way it looks out on the bare feet of sand that parts it from the sea, gives the sense that it is almost alive. That it sees something out there, where the waves break in the light of the white spring sun.

We lock the rented bikes outside and enter the last building on our tour of the island, which unlike the others does not have a Japanese name, but the French title of Les Archives du Cœur. The archives of the heart.

Inside is almost clinical: three rooms, different functions. Behind a glass partition an elderly Japanese man in a fedora sits in a chair, wires trailing from the exposure of his open shirt to a recording device, which seems to be registering the beat of his heart. On seeing us attempt to peer in through the openings of the venetian blinds, a woman in a pale blue smock stands and twists a glass wand to the side. White slats shutter: the glass opaque, though we still hear, very faintly, the sound of the heart.

'This way, please,' a woman says to us, and leads us to a door marked Heart Room. When she opens it, there is nothing but black. And the sound, far off, of a heart, under glass, pounding its affirmation. We look at each other – unsure, excited, ready to be lost – and step into the dark.

*

The words echo into the auditorium: along velvet seats, over the heads of state dignitaries, up into the upper level where booths of smoked glass secret away people just like her, caught somewhere between an earpiece and a microphone. In that space where words turn themselves inside out. Below her, Nakayoshi Hirokazu speaks to the assembled representatives of the United Nations. The representatives do not hear him; the words spill out, crash over them in waves. They wait for her to speak, even though they can't see her, even though they will act as though the words came from the man at the lectern. They wait for her to speak for him. Six seconds. This is the delay in translation.

It is a peculiar sensation. It's easier for her to move between European languages, which for her have always seemed like coins: one side on the other, the words glued together at the back – *je*-I, speak-*sprachen*. One of the other interpreters, a German speaker originally from Romania, told her that German is the same as Japanese, that a speaker must wait till the end of a sentence for the rest to make sense, just as she does now, waiting for Nakayoshi to reach where the verb hides itself. She waits to snap shut the whole flux of his sentence, built of predicative phrases, honorific verb forms, the full stop of a particle. How is she supposed to convey this man's inappropriately masculine phrasing? His aggressive interjections closed by a final *ze*? She hesitates, letting the subject float free: *I...* she says, though the word is not her own.

How wonderful it would be, she thinks, to erase his I beneath hers, make him sound, in English, like a mewling schoolboy, addressing himself politely to a stern schoolmarm. Serve him right. No one should be speaking the way he is in politics. But it is the golden rule: the translator does not lie.

She resigns herself to this peculiar dislocation, as if opening a small part of her, like a shoulder from a socket, except it isn't bone or cartilage, but whatever delicate tissue language is comprised of. The words flow through her, linger on her tongue even when she has cast them into the void of the microphone, down into the earpieces of the audience below. He speaks, she speaks. The audience waits. Six seconds. She feels the words, spits them out. When Nakayoshi finally steps down, she has lost all sense of time. Looking at the different clocks around the room, she cannot tell which one is now.

A Korean man steps up to the podium and addresses the congregation in French, thanking the esteemed representatives for attending. Here she unstitches the words and rearranges them into Japanese, this time rendering it somewhat prim, a little cold. Something to show Nakayoshi how a real politician should sound.

On the train home, she pushes her headphones in until her ears ache. No music. Just two hours of surf. Even then, a few snippets of words, a few fragments, still intrude in her skull. Not her voice. Masculine *ze*'s zip to and fro in her head. French nouns with Korean vowels sit in it like blowfish, too swollen to get back out the thin channel of her ear. She tries to focus on the quiet pouring into her, the sway of the train. People who are not her converse in her brain.

When she gets home, an email from her supervisor is waiting in her inbox, telling her there have been complaints about the work she did that day.

Some of the foreign representatives, it reads, *felt that your English was over-aggressive. Nakayoshi-san has also been in touch to tell us that he felt the Japanese you used was overly polite. In fact, he felt as if you were belittling him. He has asked us to remind you of your position.*

She sighs. How could they forget the golden rule?

She hadn't planned on going tonight; she was trying to cut back, to prove to herself that she could. But rereading the e-mail she realises just how much she needs it. Something stirs in her. She grabs her coat and goes out in the night, in search of the archive.

*

The Heart Room beats. As soon as the woman closes the door behind us, shutting out the last sliver of natural light, it starts: pounding, deep as earthquakes. Then light. Bulbs of strange contortion, the glass bare, pulses in time with a cat-purr bass. Heartbeats. Loud and from all sides, thudding through us, our eyes in the dark stunned by the flash of light that accompanies them. There is nothing else in the room. It is a small space around which we walk, dazed, in the sound of another living being.

Then it changes. Another heart begins to pulse, this time different to the first, yet common. We stay there, wandering in circles, as the hearts change places, transfer, communicate, in their own way, a message in which we find ourselves lost.

The lights flash: on and off, open, shut. I can't help but feel that this is what it must feel like to be nestled in the chamber of a heart, the light controlled only by the Morse code of aorta, the opening of ventricles, and the wet thud of the rhythm that sustains it.

*

It's getting harder to keep track of who he is meant to be, of who he is and where. Cockney to the woman at the shops, Irish to his neighbours. He bumps into a man on the street by mistake and apologises in a thick Dutch accent. At the laundromat, he is glad of the thrum of the machines, thudding heart-like, washing away any need for speech in lavender froth and seminal bleach.

Laundry day is his favourite day. He savours the quiet, the soapsuds drowning out all other voices. This late in the evening, there is no one else there except a woman with her head wrapped in a gold head-tie, reading a Kazuo Ishiguro paperback while a small child sleeps in her lap and another peers into the washers, marvelling at the ocean crashing against their plastic porthole.

'Mum,' he shouts.

'Hush, now,' she replies, without taking her eyes from the page peeled up in one of her hands, ready to move seamlessly to the next. 'Don't shout, it is rude.'

The clipped constants and long vowels drift into him, settle in his head with the sensation of cheese wire pressed against gums. He doesn't seek them out any more, these voices. At the start he had, had ridden the bus all day listening to people speak, taking notes (rhotic, non-rhotic, diphthong-heavy, first-language interference). But now they settle in him like a house settles. It is all he can do to keep them under control, to remember where and when he speaks and as whom. When he speaks to himself in the mirror, he can no longer remember which voice is his. Is it the Northern Irish, the Doric, the Israeli, Castellano? He searches his face for a hint but the features there are so unremarkable, so sallow, he could be Spanish or North African, Scandinavian with liver failure. Is that him, the Icelandic one? He can no longer remember.

The child is pulling at flyers on a corkboard. Washing machine for sale. Flat for let. Women's names and taxi numbers. Advertisements. Three months ago now since he called a number on that board offering accent training for actors. A way up the ladder. Another skill on the CV. Maybe he would finally get something more than a bit part. Finally break through. And it had helped, at first. Before he started losing himself in the roles. And now he doesn't even have to act for it to happen: all he has to do is hear a voice and he loses his own.

The boy pulls a flyer off the corkboard and the green pushpins scatter on the linoleum.

'Aremi,' the mother scolds. 'Come away.'

The child runs by the window; its reflection chases after it. Outside is night: the glass makes thing doubled, tripled, indistinguishable. He feels something out there in the dark, the way one feels an animal in the undergrowth. But when had he ever been in a forest? There are none in this city, and he cannot remember how he knows this, but something flashes in his mind, of a man with red hair holding a bag of blackberries and a dog running into the woods and a warning he can't quite remember.

His laundry comes to a stop; he puts his hand into the warm clothes, which look like so many parts of bodies – a torso of shirt, a foot of sock – that for a minute he feels entirely disarticulate. It feels good; it feels free. Seeing the woman staring at him, he gathers up his clothes, puts them in the bag and leaves as fast as he can. He wishes her a good night as he walks through the door. Her eyes widen in offence. The voice is a perfect imitation of her own.

*

After the Heart Room, the woman who led us through asks if we would like to record our own hearts to take part in the exhibit. I decline; my partner consents gladly.

In the room where moments before we saw a frail gentleman let a nurse record his heart, I watch the same nurse move to apply recording instruments under my partner's T-shirt, only for him to tear the thing off entirely, unabashedly revealing a white appendectomy scar and the skin where his tan fades in lines as soft as coasts. The nurse seems appalled by this sudden undress.

'I'm going to go wander,' I say, wanting to remove myself from the embarrassment I feel where he doesn't.

'All right,' he says, rolling his eyes, aware of my unease.

Aside from the Heart Room and the Recording Room, there is the Archive: a small computer containing information on all the hearts, with a pair of headphones gently tangled to the side. Somehow, shorn of the immediacy they possessed in the Heart Room, the heartbeats sound sadder, more forlorn, in this well-appointed office space with its already out-of-date computer. I take the headphones off and scroll through the records while I wait for him to be done. Some of the comments simply say things like 'Alfonzo Riviera, 47. New York' while others say 'heart transplanted in 1997' or even 'passed in 2004'. Had any of the hearts we had heard been those of dead men, dead women? Who does a heart belong to once transplanted?

'I heard there's more of these, you know,' a voice says. It comes from beyond the window, open just enough to let a cool breeze stir the municipal air of the archive. I push it open further and crane to listen.

'Really? I thought this was the only installation.'

'No, no, this is the only one that's *official*.' The voice is female, but the accent is somewhere between the Atlantic and the Pacific. Some stripe of American, I assume. 'But apparently there are pirated copies of this.'

'Why would anyone do that? I mean, it's cool, but I wouldn't go as far as to steal it.' The second voice is male, slightly younger than the first.

'Well,' the first voice says. I imagine the speaker leaning closer to the ear of the second, just as I lean closer to the window to make it out. 'It's some shady business where people go and pay to have a kind of psychedelic experience, an out-of-body kind of thing, or maybe it's sex and they get off on it. I don't know. But I heard Audie telling Gene about a girl she works with that goes to one. She doesn't really talk about it, but she's seen her going at night, ducking into an alley when she was walking just a bit in front of her on the way to the bus home after work. Shame, really. The girl's

Brazilian and it's her first time away from home and she gets caught up in all that business.'

'Sex?' the second voice asks. 'From this? I don't know. I guess it's kind of... intimate but not *that* intimate. I found it more... I don't know – dissociative? Like I kind of forgot who I was for a second.'

'Maybe that's what they get off on.'

'Maybe.'

'Hey, babe, what are you doing?' This voice familiar, booming from the door behind me. The voices outside the window stop.

'I'll tell you on the way home,' I say, putting the head-phones on as I sit back into the seat. Daniel MacLean, 23. Passed in '02. His heart beats loud and insistent in my ears, for all the world as if the organ had survived him.

*

There are no words. This is the best bit. This feeling she has as she steps behind a sheet of clear vinyl, into a room lit only by dim bulbs in bare cages. The air holds the metallic edge of blood. Far off in the building she hears the lowing of beasts. She has never questioned why this place should be housed within the recesses of a kosher butcher, or why she should need to come round the back, through the alley where the blood runs out, why she should knock three times on the door and wait for it to open. But she does it, without knowing why. And there are no words. None.

A young woman with six hoops in her ear and an Afro cut into soft spikes sits at the reception, if you could even call it that. A barrier taller than her head stops her seeing all but the woman's head and shoulders. They look at each other; the woman smiles in recognition, and says nothing. She would mistake this as a sign of intimacy had it not been the same the first time she came, so many years ago, driven through a late November night in the rain to find this place, voices that didn't belong to her howling in her ears. Sanctuary, this is what she considers this place. The word comes to her in English – there is no concept of sanctuary in Japanese. She can say it as *seiki*, which recalls only the old meaning, of a holy place. If she means it politically, she has to use the word *hinansho*, a place where one flees danger. Between the two words the sense of a secret gets lost. But this place is, for her, somewhere secret, holy, and safe, all at once. *Sanctuary*, she thinks, savouring the crispness of the consonants, as the woman rises from behind the desk and leads her by the hand into the dark.

It is intimate; somewhere between a doctor's examination and sex, how this woman takes her limbs in her strong, smooth fingers – fingers that have disappeared in the dark, transformed now into only the smell of cocoa butter and fresh nail polish – and places her in a large leather chair. The leather is soft and supple; she recalls the bovine sounds elsewhere in the buildings, but here, in the heart of it, there is only silence, total darkness.

A large pair of padded headphones are placed over her ears. There is hissing in the dark; without sight she sees snakes, pouring from somewhere, imagines them crawling over her. And then it kicks in: what she has been waiting for, that sound, from everywhere at once, thrumming in her bones. The beat of a heart. Her own, channelled through a microphone affixed to her chest by an electrode pad. Not a stranger's. Not a dead heart. Not a pig's heart sewn into a human body. Not a heart part plastic, pumping minerals with odd valves and strange pressures. But her, her own heart, present in each bright flush of crimson. She listens. The heart speaks nothing but itself, its pounding insistence. And it is impossible to translate.

*

After the quiet of the islands in the West, I had expected Tokyo to be nothing but noise: the shrill ring of an arcade game, subway announcements, cries of hawkers before the neon pavilions of all-night karaoke. But some change has occurred in the week since our arrival in Japan, somewhere between the train station bento and late night sashimi and ordering in restaurants by pointing at pictures. The Japanese language, until then impenetrable, has started crumble. As if some wall of sound, now in new light, has begun to show its bricks, and piece by piece, be taken apart. The fragments swirl: *konnichiwa, irashaimase, kashikomari-mashita*. Meaningless. Other people's voices repeat in my mind, and though I try to keep them quiet, to banish them with English phrases like *how do you do* and *some weather we've having*, or when that doesn't work, *I am I am I am*, nothing seems to help. I don't mention it for fear of ruining the holiday. Instead I eat ibuprofen from our first-aid kit when the headaches get too much, and try to enjoy our last week abroad.

Shibuya on our last night, a Macanese restaurant with Tiki torches and oversized hyacinths painted on the walls. The waiter eyes us nervously from across the room, afraid of another interaction where language fails us all. Every time we make to order he gestures for a woman to come speak to us in English. My partner orders another bottle of wine and says *arigatō* to her bowed head. I see her smile as she walks away, amused by this small gesture of humility.

'I can't stop thinking,' he says, washing papaya salad down with the last of the wine, 'about what you said that woman was saying about there being other *archives du cœur.*' This last he says with no approximation of the French, in keeping with his middle-class comfort with mistakes. 'I mean, it was great. A really... I don't know, I guess it was kind of intimate, if you can even say that. But it made me feel close to whoever's heart it was. I just can't help thinking what kind of people would want that experience. Who would need it?'

'I was looking through the recordings,' I say. 'A lot of those hearts are dead now. And some were transplants. It's strange, isn't it? That you could feel close to a dead heart, or one that wasn't somebody else's to begin with. I mean, I guess the point of the exhibit is that it does that, makes you feel close, but it only works because we assume the heart is... key. But you know how we point to our chests when we say *who, me?* Well, in Japan they apparently point at the nose.'

The waiter comes over and refills our glasses, whispering *shitsurei shimasu* so as not to disturb us. Still, the words get recorded; some device in my head picks them up whether I want it to or not, and proceeds to hit play. The words repeat, pulse, alive. I gasp the freshly poured wine.

'Easy,' he says. 'You don't want to be hungover for the flight.'

'I just wish we were home already.'

'But it's been good, though, hasn't it?'

'It has,' I say. 'But we've been gone too long. I'm ready for creature comforts. English, again.'

'But it's such an adventure, isn't it? Everywhere we

go these days, everyone speaks English. It's hard to get a sense that you're anywhere else. McDonald's, Starbucks, it's the same on Lexington as it is in Milan. I like being here,' he says. 'You get the idea that you're actually somewhere different. That anything could happen.'

'I suppose,' I say. 'But you feel comfortable anywhere you go. It's harder for other people to be far from home.'

He puts his hand over mine.

'Home is where the heart is, babe,' he says.

Sometimes it feels as though we speak different languages.

*

It is raining: lush, cinematic rain. He folds his laundry in the dark, listening to the water beat its quiet hush and how it turns the cars on the street into nothing but sighs. The white noise fills his head like balm. By the time he has balled the last of his socks and put them away, he is calm, almost. In the dark of the flat, he feels once more himself. In part, at least.

The phone rings.

It's me, says a woman on the other end. He knows he should know her, but the voice is lost in the others in his head, labelled, somewhere, in the dark recesses where memory is kept. He speaks with her accent. This one feels different, as if it, or something very close to it, might have belonged to him, once. She tells him about people he thinks he knows, would remember, surely, if he saw them. But at this distance it seems as though they are far away, in another place. When the call is over and they say goodbye, he cannot remember what was said, or how the voice sounded. In the dark, he tries to resurrect it, imitate himself. He can't remember it, no matter how hard he tries. All the other ones come to take its place: the woman from the laundromat, the Irish man on the bus, Canadian, Filipino, South Korean, Thai, Geordie, New Haven, Glasgow, Qatar. The voice he had used on the phone is inaccessible, though it is the only one he wants to remember.

The flat is too quiet, his mind too hot. He goes out into the night, umbrella in hand. The raindrops bounce and scatter on the taut vinyl. The streets are deserted. Most of the shops have closed, only a few restaurants still shine their lights across the slick macadam and concrete. He has no stomach for food, or for liquor, or for anything, really. He simply wanders, feeling as though there is something out there he has to find. Is this how a junkie finds a score, he wonders, by some compass embedded in the veins? He walks in circles, avoids the subway, compelled to keep going until, eventually, he finds himself in a back alley, with a large open grille, and the smell of old blood almost hidden beneath the rich scent of petrichor. There is a door: a Japanese woman emerges from it, her hair slick with rain in a matter of seconds. She looks at him, quickly, then averts her eyes and moves off into the night, as if ashamed to have been seen here. He feels something pass between them, some small affinity, but then she is gone.

He knocks on the door, three times, though he doesn't know why. It opens. The path inside is dark, and no one else is there to guide him, only the low cries of cows off somewhere in the distance. He wanders until he comes upon a room, behind a sheet of clear vinyl, lit by strange bulbs and lacking furniture save a high desk, behind which a woman sits. She looks at him and smiles. It feels almost scandalously intimate. As if she knows him. As if she understands. He expects her to speak, but instead she simply smiles, gets up, takes him by the hand and leads him off into the dark, where he listens to the persistent thrum of something living, some animal vibration. It speaks something to him: something he cannot mimic, something he can barely understand, but which, with each shudder of aorta and myocardium, reminds him of who he is, or who he was meant to be. Who he might have been, once.

*

People come and go. The visits last about twenty minutes, roughly; I keep time with my watch, which tells me I should be going back to the hotel room soon, before he wakes without me and worries. But I find it hard to pry myself away from keeping watch on this public bath in a Yotsuya back alley, where men and women have been coming and going now for four hours, at least, and most likely long before I found it on a sleepless walk around the hotel, trying to cast the Japanese words from my head – *shitsurei shimasu*, the waiter says, over and over, *irasshaimase*.

What do they come here for? How do they even know about this place?

A stupid question. I know they must feel what I feel – a kind of pull, like magnetism. I take a drink of the iced coffee I picked up at a convenience store, and a bite of curry pan as I check my watch. A man emerges from the doorway looking satisfied. At first, I thought this place was a brothel or a drug den, maybe, but considering the variety of the clientele it seems to me now that it must be something else. Not to mention that strange pull. Another glance at the watch. 5.40. We have to be out of the hotel by seven to make our flight. But how can I leave without seeing for myself?

A look down the street. No one else is coming. Perhaps it is too late, or perhaps there is a lull in appointments. Had the people even made appointments? Another five minutes and still no one. I steel myself. 5.47. It's now or never.

The deep blue cloth on the entrance peels back with a flutter. A water feature burbles in a reception area of pale wood and green cushions, while a white egg puffs citrus vapour at an interval of six seconds. A man is sitting on a chair behind a desk.

He looks at me and smiles. It is shockingly intimate; as if he has known me my entire life, as if he knows me in a way I do not. Better. He smiles, stands, reaches his hand out and takes mine. And there are no words. Quiet blossoms in my head, big soft clouds of it. Not a single word as he leads me deeper into this building that I recognise, now, whose function I think I can understand.

There is a seat, headphones, an electrode pad glued to a chest. But there are no words. And I think, as the headphones slide over me, about all those people who came here before, about the other archives, out there somewhere, disguised as bath houses and tattoo parlours and butchers' yards, about the people who go there, who need them. How to describe it? The need for this pulse that is my own fed back to me, for this thudding, this message relayed in heartbeats like the galloping of some beast. I can't. There are no words. And that's the best bit – there are no words, here, in the heart of the archive.

In Ribbons

'It's fox-work,' Hiro's grandmother says, her eyes gleaming like jaspers, her thin fingers winding a needle through thinner cloth, closing a rift in Father's shirt. Each week Grandma washes the clothes so hard her knuckles redden, but still some specks of coal dust twine themselves into the weave.

'Don't be ridiculous,' says his mother. 'It was just a gas leak in the shaft.'

Grandma snorts. Mother rolls her eyes.

'When did they say the doctor'd get here?' Mother asks, this time turning toward Father, prone on a floor cushion and veiled in tobacco smoke.

'A proper medical doctor's coming from the city tomorrow,' he says, running a hand along his forearms in search of dirt. His nail beds keep the minerals of the mine: coal dust and mud ground so deep they would never be clean again. But still Father washes his hands before dinner, and at night, searches his skin for scrap metal. That he will be filthy again tomorrow doesn't seem to matter, so long as he can go to bed clean, or very close to it. 'The pit-doctor's done what he can for him for now, says he can't be moved, needs special medicine, the kind they don't keep around here.'

This elicits no response. The shack is quiet tonight, without Grandpa, the shadows in the room darker. No one seems to want to talk: Grandma darns, Mother cleans, Father smokes. An animal scratches at the outside of the wall.

When Mother and Father get ready for bed, Grandma calls Hiro to her side.

'Listen to Grandma,' she whispers as she runs her fingers through his hair. 'Grandpa needs special medicine.'

'I know,' Hiro says. 'Papa said the doctor will come tomorrow.'

'Your papa is a good man, Hiro,' she says. 'But stupid. Modern. Grandpa needs special medicine and he needs it tonight. I would go get it, but your grandma's too old to go out in the dark now. The things out there don't have a taste for children, but an old lady like me, they would gobble right up.'

Hiro looks up at grandma's face: the lines worn deep in it, the way her mouth goes wide as she speaks in pure *Chikuhō-ben*. His mother and father speak the dialect too, but softer. When they talk to the mine officials they use a kind of Japanese Grandma never uses, one she calls 'standard' and punctuates with a spit. Is Grandma old? He has never thought about it. To Hiro, Grandma is Grandma. No more, no less.

'I need you to go see Miss Pak,' she says, gripping his arm.

Hiro's skin pebbles under Grandma's insistent fingers.

Miss Pak lives in a different part of the *naiyō*, the little mining town where Hiro lives with his family. Around Hiro's house there are mainly Japanese from different areas of Kyushu, some from farther abroad, and one or two Koreans. Where Miss Pak lives it is mainly Koreans and some Taiwanese. He doesn't need light to find his way there in the dark; at night the Koreans sing songs, different ones to the other miners, in a language that sounds like elastic pinging.

Miss Pak's house is easy to find: you just need to follow the smell of tea. Hard as it is to procure in the *naiyō*, Miss Pak always has a supply of quality *genmai cha*. She often brings some when she comes to see Grandma, and the two sit there, gossiping in thick *Chikuhō-ben*, the shack warm with the smell of toasted rice wafting from the iron kettle. Miss Pak brings tea for Grandma, and a piece of candy for Hiro. It isn't that he doesn't like Miss Pak. But she scares him. It's her eyes. Clouded, as if the sky moves in them, and though Miss Pak is completely blind, she gets around the *naiyō* with no assistance, not even a stick, as she walks past the machinery, the gambling dens, and the house near the bar where only women live. Hiro doesn't understand why, but whenever he walks through the *naiyō* with his mother, her step quickens past this house. When he walks with Grandma she takes her time and says hello to the women who live there, coming and going at all times of day.

He has asked Grandma how Miss Pak came to be blind, but each time, Grandma shook her head and said, 'There are some things little boys shouldn't know.'

He follows the smell of toasted rice past the women's house and through the Korean songs. A few men stumble in the streets, but Grandma has told him no one in the *naiyō* would ever hurt a little boy – far more dangerous to be a woman, young or old, in this day and age, she said.

He walks the dirt path of the *naiyō*, making sure to stick to the lighted parts, as Grandma taught him. The air is

71

warm with the smell of *genmai cha*, the night heavy with song. The *naiyō* has never felt dangerous before. But tonight. He feels as though he is not alone. Somewhere in the distance, he hears an animal scratching, as he takes the last few steps to Miss Pak's door.

One of Miss Pak's granddaughters greets him on the porch. Miss Pak has many granddaughters; or so, at least, it seems to Hiro. They all call her *harumoni*, which Grandma told him meant 'grandma' in Korean. The young woman leads him into the house, calling out softly in that language of elastic. *Harumoni* is the only word he recognises.

For a minute he thinks he is back home: the frail old woman sitting by the fire, the iron kettle in the hearth. He mistakes her for his grandma. But his heart stops when he sees the eyes: as if someone had poured milk into tea, like the foreigners did, and now it roils there, unable to be still.

'Hiro,' she says. 'Why are you here so late at night? Is your grandma OK?'

'She's OK, Miss Pak,' he says. 'It's Grandpa. There was an explosion at the mine. Grandma says he needs special medicine.'

Miss Pak narrows her eyes and looks straight at Hiro. His skin pebbles under her gaze.

'Is that so?' she asks. 'Did your grandma say anything else?'

He shuffles his feet, embarrassed. His mother had told him never to listen to his grandma's stories. His parents tried to stop her, wave the words away, tell her not to fill his head with nonsense, each time she told him about the creatures of the high mountain – the ogres, the crag-hags, the foxes. He doesn't want to seem silly, doesn't want to seem like a little boy, in front of Miss Pak and her granddaughters.

'Grandma says,' he begins, but seeing three of Miss Pak's granddaughters in the room, darning, others massaging muscles sore from working all day in the mine, stretching their jaws to loosen muscles stiff from holding lanterns in their mouths, his voice quivers and breaks.

'Out with it, Hiro,' Miss Pak says, admonishing the women's laugher with a raised hand.

'Grandma says it's fox-work,' he says, his cheeks burning.

The room goes still. The only sound is the crackling of the fire, the sound of something scratching, and the gentle pull of a needle in cloth, the work that will not stop for something as small as this. Miss Pak stands up, goes to a small chest of drawers, and begins to pull out various powders and liquids. These she pours into a mortar and grinds with a pestle. The paste she wraps in a banana leaf and ties with a red ribbon, the same kind, Hiro notes, she uses to tie her hair back. She tucks the package into her carry pouch. Without any assistance; as if even blind, she knows exactly where each thing should be. Hiro worries that maybe she's made a mistake in making her medicine. For some reason he can't explain, he thinks he would prefer a Japanese doctor.

'Sun-Hwa,' she calls to one of her granddaughters. 'Fetch my coat. Hiro, take me to your grandpa.'

Walking the town with Miss Pak is a very different experience to walking it alone, or even with Grandma. People call out to her, men and women, in Korean and Japanese, all of them respectfully, no matter how drunk they might be – and some of them are quite drunk tonight – or how much they are rushing to other engagements. Miss Pak, for her part, bows her head deferentially at each greeting, replies, but never lets her stride falter. One foot in front of the other

73

on the muddy ground of the *naiyō*, without so much as a stumble. Hiro is uneasy. It is as if the old blind woman is leading him, rather than him guiding her through the night.

There is something about the increased visibility of walking with Miss Pak. As if Miss Pak's presence draws not just the respect of the residents of the *naiyō*, but something else. Something that lies just at the edge of lamplight, hungry and waiting.

'You feel them out there, don't you,' Miss Pak says as they take the corner toward the mine's makeshift hospital.

'What are they?' Hiro asks.

'Foxes,' she says. 'Wild foxes. They shouldn't be so close. Something must have disturbed them.'

'But Miss Pak,' Hiro says. 'Mr Watanabe says that foxes are good. They're the servants of the goddess Inari.'

Miss Pak snorts; it is eerily similar to the way his grandmother snorts when his mother tries to tell her one of her stories is nonsense.

'The grocer? What would he know about anything?' Miss Pak asks. 'There are foxes here in Chikuhō that were never domesticated by the Japanese gods, Hiro. You remember that. There were things here long before Japan.'

The last she says in a strange tone; almost sad.

They walk the rest of the way to the hospital in silence. And the entire time, Hiro feels those eyes on him, closer as they approach the hospital. He feels something in the night. Something hard and sharp, focused. A hunger so large it would swallow him up. But every time Miss Pak looks out into the dark, it seems to lessen. As if it too cannot bear to be under that blind gaze.

Grandpa is wrapped in bandages and laid out on the floor.

The ends of the bandages have been tied up in a bow. The white linen has been soaked with blood and lymph. Parts of it are stained orange and crack when Miss Pak moves him. Grandpa stays asleep the entire time, his eyes flickering in the grip of whatever dream the pit-doctor's medicine has put him under. Hiro thinks that maybe he should tell Miss Pak to look out for the places where the bandages are wet with excretion, but for some reason, as she runs her hands over them, not caring what her fingers touch, Hiro feels embarrassed about doing so.

'Is he going to die?' Hiro asks instead.

'He might,' Miss Pak replies. 'But he might live, too. These things no one can tell. Not even wise old women like me and your grandmother.'

The last she says with a wink. Hiro smiles. This is the longest he has ever spent with Miss Pak, and though he still feels strange when he sees her eyes, his skin no longer pebbles. The hospital room isn't much; a supply closet with one window, through which pale moonlight streams, the rest lit by mine lights – *kantera* – which look like tea kettles but are filled with oil, a lit wick in their spouts making the sickroom glow. It isn't much. But it's the best they can do. The doctor and nurse that treat the mineworkers have gone home for the night, but still Miss Pak urged Hiro to be quiet as a mouse as they moved through the building to get here.

Miss Pak lifts the banana-leaf package halfway from her pouch then lets it fall back. She tilts her head to the side and listens. Hiro is about to ask her what's wrong when he hears it too: the sound of footsteps coming from outside.

'Hide,' Miss Pak commands. Hiro does so without thinking, only realising, once he has crouched down between two beds at the back of the room, that there's no reason they shouldn't be there. He peeks out from the gap between the beds and tries to find Miss Pak, but she too has secreted herself somewhere in the storeroom-cum-medical bay.

A man's shadow fills the doorway. When he steps into the light of the *kantera*, Hiro sees that he is a doctor: a long white coat, and an armband with the Japanese imperial insignia, marks him as a military doctor. The doctor from the mainland must have come earlier than expected. Hiro moves to come out of the shadow, but something stops him: an imagined compulsion from Miss Pak. Silent words she has mouthed in the dark. He stays crouched, and watches as the doctor approaches his grandfather's prone body.

The doctor first does what Miss Pak had done: he takes each of Grandpa's limbs, examines them, runs his hands along them. Grandpa groans; the doctor's touch is not as delicate as Miss Pak's. The doctor leans down and whispers something in Grandpa's ear. Grandpa stills. The doctor begins to untie the bandages, unwrapping long ribbons of linen, unpeeling it from its sediment in molten skin and patchwork scab. Grandpa has no reaction. It is as if the doctor has put him into a sleep so deep not even pain can penetrate. What a deep sleep it must be, Hiro thinks. Deeper than the mineshafts of the deepest pit, where Grandma says the wild foxes play, making fires in the tunnels, and eating miners who go astray. Women are safest in the mines, Grandma said, because they carry their children with them, and the foxes won't eat babies. They like to wait for them to grow big first, she said. The foxes were, first and foremost, very, very smart. How deep a sleep it must be. The sleep of the foxes in the deep caves. Do the foxes sing songs like the miners do? The minecarts' braying – *goton goton* – as percussion.

The doctor is still unwinding bandages. Except now Hiro sees that the linen is in a pile on the floor, next to the doctor's feet. But the doctor is still unwinding something from his grandpa. Something long and red. Skin. The doctor is peeling Grandpa's skin off in ribbons: long swathes of it unravelling in his hands like the peel of an apple, round and round in the doctor's hands, denuding Grandpa's already naked flesh. The end of the strip the doctor places in his mouth and begins to chew, gulping it down even as he tears more off. The room is filled with the wet sound of skin ground in molars, and the scratch, scratch as the doctor rips at the skin. Hiro tries to move but his limbs won't comply. He cannot force his legs to carry him into the circle of *kantera* light. It is Miss Pak who steps into the circle.

The doctor turns round and stares at her, a strip of skin still in his hands and mouth. Miss Pak says nothing, just fixes him with her blind gaze.

The doctor swallows a mouthful of Grandpa's skin and places the loose end of it back on his torso. He unsteadily moves sideways, eyes trained on Miss Pak. Miss Pak's sightless eyes follow him wherever he goes.

'I see you,' Miss Pak says.

He lunges at her. Miss Pak grabs a *kantera* and brings it down over his head, spilling lit oil out of the kettle spout and over the man. Oil splashes down his long coat. He barks in pain, and his face, in the burning light, seems more pointed, longer, vulpine. He runs around the room, trying to find the exit he has forgotten in his pain, trying to find Miss Pak's throat, but she has another *kantera* in her hand, and each time he gets close, she waves the fire in front of her and drives him back. Eventually he finds the door and runs out of it, doubled over in pain, on all fours like a dog.

When he is gone, Miss Pak stands still for a moment, taking deep breaths, the *kantera* burning at her side. Then she moves to Hiro's grandpa and picks up the ribbon of skin. Retrieving a pair of scissors from her pouch, she snips the length of it and lets the rest fall on the floor with the bandages. She then takes her banana-leaf wrapper, cuts the ribbon, and uses her fingers to apply the paste to the areas where the skin has been burnt and peeled. Dead skin sheds under her fingers, like a snake, moulting. Once she has applied all of the salve, she leans on the table, suddenly exhausted.

'All right, Hiro,' she calls. 'Come out, now.'

Shaking as he crawls out from his hiding space, Hiro says, 'We owe you a thousand packets of *genmai cha*, Miss Pak.'

Miss Pak laughs. 'Oh no, child. For some things, there is no price. No matter what people tell you. Remember this, even if you remember nothing else about tonight.'

Hiro doesn't understand. Unsure what to say, he helps the blind lady rebandage his grandpa's naked body. Hiro looks away when she covers the genitals and the areas where the skin has been peeled back to show quivering muscle. Miss Pak does not: she simply looks on, blindly, as she rewraps the old man. The entire time, he does not stir. Simply sleeps that deep sleep, a sleep deeper than pits.

The doctor – the real one, the specialist – comes from Fukuoka the next day. He wears a waxed leather trench coat that catches the mud of the *naiyō* as he walks through; droplets of it cling to him and slide off with each step. On his lapel he wears a pin in the shape of the Japanese flag. Once he arrives at the hospital, and after much persuasion, mostly from Grandma, he permits the family to be present for the treatment. When he unwraps Grandpa's bandages to look below, he makes a small disgusted sound.

'What is this?' he asks. 'Some folk remedy? You country folk. You really need to stop thinking you know anything about medicine. It doesn't look like you've done any damage, but you're damn lucky.'

Grandma says something the doctor doesn't understand – the dialect is too strong. It is a word Hiro doesn't know, but when he sees his parents' faces turn scarlet, he knows it is a bad word. The doctor resumes his treatment, but seems unsettled. As if he can feel Grandma's eyes boring into his back while he works on her husband.

'Quite remarkable,' he says. 'And you say the explosion was yesterday? The man is a fine example of the Japanese spirit. His skin has already started to grow back. He'll be back in the mine in no time.'

The doctor uses the word *tenkō* for mine, instead of the word *yama* everyone in the *naiyō* uses. For some reason, when he says it, it makes the mine seem like a different place; somewhere very far away. Hiro is surprised to find that, when the doctor speaks, his skin pebbles.

A week later, skin still in bandages, Grandpa goes back into the pit.

Two weeks after Grandpa returns to the mine, Miss Pak dies. One of her granddaughters finds her, what is left of her.

Hiro had not seen Miss Pak since the incident; he had been trying very hard to forget it, to blur it, to consider it a bad dream or a trick of the *kantera*'s shifting light. And yet when he bunches his eyes, and tries very hard to forget, he feels as though Miss Pak is looking at him with those milk-tea irises.

There are whispers around the *naiyō* about the state in which Miss Pak was found. Some say there were chunks of her body torn out, as if by a wild animal. Others that she was murdered by a former lover, from her youth, when she had been quite the beauty. Some even said that when they found her body, she had been completely skinless, as if she had been spun round and peeled like an apple. This last makes a chill leak into Hiro's bones. The same chill you find in the mine, in the deep pits, when someone cracks rock only to find a surge of ice water, filling the shaft with the kind of cold that leaves the men, and Hiro, shivering for days.

Two nights after Miss Pak's death, Grandma wakes Hiro in the middle of the night, urges him to dress, and bustles him out into the night, a *kantera* in her hand.

'We're going to repay Miss Pak for what she did for us,' Grandma says.

'Miss Pak said not to repay her,' Hiro says, rubbing his knuckles in his eyes. 'Said some things have no price.'

He sees Grandma's eyes widen in the night; the light of the *kantera* spout glitters in them like stars.

'Miss Pak is a smart woman,' Grandma says. 'Was.'

Her voice threatens to break as she corrects herself.

They make their way to the mountainside, into the forest that still stands where the wood hasn't been cleared for the *naiyō* or the slag heaps of the pit. The *kantera* light makes the shadows between the trees seem to run alongside them. Hiro clings to his grandmother's hand. And yet tonight, she does not tell him that he will be safe, that the night has no taste for little boys. She grips his hand in turn and hoists the *kantera*, refusing to take her eyes off the path she is making through the woods. Hiro thinks her pace might be quickening. The shadows race faster. Closer.

It is only when the trees give way to a clearing filled with light that Hiro realises he had been holding his breath. He is even more surprised to hear his grandmother let out her own breath next to him.

'Well done, Hiro,' she says, though he hasn't done anything. 'Now you need to do some work.'

Miss Pak's granddaughters stand in the clearing in black *hanbok* dresses. Others are there too, some obviously Korean, others Japanese, though fewer by far. The women outnumber the men.

'What is this, Grandma?'

'A funeral, Hiro.'

'Are we going to burn Miss Pak?'

'No, Hiro. The Koreans bury their dead. We are here to bury her, and to pay our respects. Go help the men dig the grave.'

Hiro nods and goes to a small patch of land that is being carved out by three Korean men and one Japanese. The work is familiar to all of them, though the eyes they feel on their back, there in the shadows of the trees, are not. As Hiro works at digging up the earth and hauling away piles of it, it feels as if he is back at work in the mine. His muscles know the motions. But tonight it is different. He has seen them burn bodies many times – accidents are daily in the pits. But he has never seen them lay one in the earth. He isn't sure what to expect. All he can think of is Miss Pak, lying there, staring up blindly at the sky. But it is not Miss Pak's body, but a large shape wrapped in linen, they lower into the grave. On its chest lies a red ribbon, tied in a bow.

Over the grave, the granddaughters speak Korean.

'Grandma,' Hiro whispers.

'Hush,' Grandma says. 'Listen.'

'But I don't understand it.'

'You don't need to understand it, Hiro. Just listen.'

They stand there, while one by one people eulogise in that language of elastic. The longer he listens, the more Hiro is sure he can feel something in the words, just at the edge of hearing. Something raw and naked. It makes him feel as if a part of himself has been torn away.

The last person to speak over the grave is Grandma. She leaves Hiro by himself with the *kantera* as she goes up to speak, in her thick *Chikuhō-ben*, about Miss Pak. For some reason, Hiro feels comforted by it. Grandma talks about how Miss Pak had been a doctor in Korea, before the army came and took her.

'She was a strong woman,' she said. 'The strongest. You had to be. To survive something like that.'

Those in the circle nod. Some are crying openly.

'What she did, I don't think any of us will ever under-stand. No matter how hard we try. What it took, what it meant, for her to do it. What it feels like to have nothing left. We say here, in the *naiyō*, we have nothing. But that isn't true; Miss Pak knew that, she knew what it was like to have nothing, to be nothing. And she survived.'

Grandma opens her mouth to say something else, but stops. She looks at Hiro, surprised, as if she had forgotten he was there.

'I am very grateful to have been able to call her my friend,' she finishes, defeated.

When people move to cover the grave, to gather the *kantera*, Hiro leads his grandma to lean on a gravestone and catch her breath. They stand there in silence for a moment.

Hiro thinks of the dead woman in the grave. Of her blind eyes.

'Grandma,' he asks. 'Will you tell me, now, how Miss Pak went blind?'

She hesitates, looks around at the people gathered there, black *hanbok* shining in the night.

'She poured nightshade in her eyes.'

'She made herself blind? Why?'

'Because it was the only way she could fight.'

'I don't understand, Grandma,' Hiro says.

The old lady twines her fingers in her grandson's hair.

'I hope you never do,' she says, and smoothes the hair she has just disturbed. 'Just remember her. That's all you can do for Miss Pak, now.'

The troupe gathers to walk back to the *naiyō*. All of them clearly unsettled by the way the shadows race around them, and the strange yips they hear out there in the dark. Then another sound. The granddaughter who had shown Hiro into Miss Pak that night begins to sing: her voice clear and thin, like a warbler. Then another, and another, the men adding their low timbre. Grandma joins, though she doesn't know the words; she sings in sound, in pitch, adding what she can to the music. Hiro adds his own voice – small as it is.

The shadows are still dark around them, rustlings still sound as they move through, strange things move in the dark. But the black does not seem so deep, filled with that song.

When they reach the *naiyō*, the groups go their separate ways, to separate parts, the town divided as it is. Each *kantera* leaves the rest darker as it departs. The shadows grow stronger. By the time Hiro and his grandma make their way alone toward the Japanese side of the *naiyō*, their *kantera* is no longer enough to keep the night at bay. The shadows shift around them, as if roused from sleep. At first, they walk fast, then unable to hold back any longer, run to the door. The shadows run with them.

Inside, at last, it is as if they have left another world behind the thick lock Grandmother slams shut behind them. The small room, the moonlight on the shapeless mounds of his sleeping parents, dead to the world. How long have they been gone?

His grandma's hands are shaking. He looks at his own and sees grave dirt buried in the nail beds.

'Time for bed, Hiro,' she says. 'It's been a long night.'

'Grandma,' he says, embarrassed. 'I don't think I can sleep. Will you tell me a story?'

The two climb into the bedding together, Hiro under Grandma's arm, and she tells him about the monsters in the high mountains, and how they live there, away from the *naiyō*, waiting. He feels safer knowing they live far away. As if the grave, Miss Pak, that night in the hospital – they all took place in another place. Far from here. And yet, as Grandma grows sleepy, and her voice wanes, another sound threatens to overtake it. From outside, against the wall. The sound of an animal. Scratching, scratching in the night.

An Easement

The leaves of Ann Arbor are scarlet and bile-yellow, crunch as we drag out to the van boxes containing: all the books Josh can't bring himself to throw away, a plastic soap dish shaped like a duck, and a set of kitchen knives my parents bought us when we moved in together. I walk round the thickest swells of leaf, Josh kicks through them in a pair of boots that once belonged to his father. Into the car we load twelve years of life packed into eight boxes.

The radio sets the pace. Michigan supplies us the jump-start required, then Indiana brings us slowly through. We listen to classic rock at the junctures of Indiana and Tennessee, Tennessee and Kentucky. By this time we have taken turns driving, drunk cherry slushies, and fooled around in the back seat, in those strange roads where the states bleed into one another. We have to keep watch for the signs that tell us we have passed the border. First one welcomes us to Arkansas, then some time after we exit, another one, bullet-marked, welcomes us to Pine Bluff.

Fourteen hours have passed since Ann Arbor. Night has settled over Arkansas. Bugs leap across the road in the sallow beams of our headlights. The wipers smear fluorescent viscera across the windscreen as we drive up to the new house.

We do not bother to unpack. Instead, Josh goes into the trunk, opens up a box, and removes some bedding, before rushing up the three stairs that lead to the front door. He unlocks it and runs back to fetch me, the bedding held in one hand while with the other he grips mine. He kicks the front door open gently to reveal the shapeless interior of our new home, the still air inside. I had imagined pitchers of iced tea, quiet light, the soft swing of porch doors. But the inside of the house feels like a held breath. The feeling of adventure that had let me leave my home in Michigan, my family, and my friends, fades in the hallway of this house in Pine Bluff. I bite my nails as Josh sets about turning on lights. I insist we sleep with them on and he accepts my childish insecurity with good grace, eager to make me feel at ease here. Even then, the dust-covered bulbs seem too little to keep back the night, which gathers itself around us like the sea, ready at any moment to scour this little house from its purchase, sweep away the little lives inside.

Josh dreams of farmland. He has always dreamed of farmland. When he was fifteen, his parents took him from Minnesota to Ann Arbor. His mother taught English at a high school across from Furstenberg Park. His father grew up on a farm, but in Michigan, worked part-time at a grocery store.

Josh preserves his parents: half his books are his mother's, filled with her tiny marginalia, which Josh uses to summon her spirit since the cancer took her.

The books fill one and a half boxes. Josh lines them up

in no real order in the bookshelves built into the walls of the upstairs study. When they are in place, he sits on the floor in front of them and stares, satisfied. This is the first furniture we put into the house: Josh's mother's corpse.

Josh's father is buried in Michigan, next to his mother. But as he looks out the study window, with the sunlight flaring the gold letters of the book spines, he seems to see something out there, in the fields around the new house. I watch him from the doorway. I wonder if, perhaps, he sees his father's body rising out of the ground, tall and thin, green as tomato stalks.

It takes us three weeks to settle properly. Objects arrive in the mail. A man brings a pale yellow refrigerator on a Tuesday, new but designed to look retro, something I bought in advance to go with my idea of our new life here. We unpack the boxes slowly, as if unsure of putting them down in this strange new place. The house agitates us; something doesn't quite fit. But when we are outside, in the fields, tending and pruning and planting, I see Josh breathe easier, knots in my back loosen. This is what we came for: the land, the making, the relief.

We tidy the cornfields, straighten the tomato stalks, plant radishes and cabbages and carrots. We plant what we can and attempt to shed the disarray gifted to us by however long this land has stood uncared for. Our hands delve the soil. Worms and beetles scurry away. Some crawl along our arms. When our hands are in the soil we feel the earth breathe.

After three weeks, the house is full of us. Our photographs are arrayed along the skirting, up the stairs. The bed is dressed. Our clothes are put away. There is a plastic soap dish shaped like a duck in the bathroom. The dark that greeted us lessens. Sometimes we see it, from the corner of our eye, in a nook where the light can't quite reach. But we have new bulbs and seeds in the soil. We will be well.

After four weeks, on a Thursday night as we get ready for bed, I stop by the window and look out at our little patch of soil. Off in the distance, at the very edge of the fields, I notice something strange: a thick line of black, like a hedgerow, but unmoving in the breeze.

'What's that?' I ask Josh. He comes over and puts his arms around me as he looks out the window.

'Just the wall,' he says. 'For the easement.'

'For what? I thought we owned the whole thing.'

'Not that part,' he says. 'The government does. Well, it does and it doesn't. It has an easement on the land, so they can use it whenever they want.'

He kisses me on the cheek. 'The house is looking good,' he whispers in my ear. 'Maybe we should think about filling it with a family.'

When we make love that night, Josh is thorough, present, as if our conversation has given him purpose. When I close my eyes all I see is the wall, out there in the dark. Splitting my home in two.

Josh took care of the paperwork, the finances. The nitty gritty. A man in Arkansas sold him a family farm for dirt cheap, or so he said. A real bargain. I thought nothing of it; just more of Josh's enthusiasm for the whole idea of moving out west. To me, Josh sold the dream of endless fields and quiet living, of our own place for a new life. When I fetch it from the bureau drawer in which we keep our papers, pays-lips, birth certificates and receipts, I scour through the bill of sale to see the nature of the deal. For a reduction in the land price of 20 per cent, the proprietor agrees, in perpetuity, to allow the use and lease of land, et cetera. Agreement A, sub-clause C, Joshua Grosvenor, hereafter party A. The United States Government. Any damages are not the liability of the US Government or any associated parties. Party A assumes all responsibility for the upkeep and maintenance, including but not limited to. All liabilities are the responsibility of party A. Fire, flood, or earthquake. Natural disaster or act of terror.

So many little things asserted in increasingly small sections of fine print. And nowhere on the document, at any point, does my name appear. I am not party to the contract, the agreement, or the easement. There is no land here that is mine, and no right of use guaranteed. For me, at least.

If we were married, perhaps this would be different. But staring at this document, signed and dated, between the government and Josh, I can't help but feel a little cheated, a little betrayed. As if Josh has been having an affair this past month, in this home we share. Which is not, technically, mine. When you get down to it. To the bottom line. To the paperwork, the finances. The nitty gritty.

Summer has not left Arkansas. The leaves cling to the trees. Their green is deep, glossy. Almost plastic. You could mistake them for props, but for the smell of them.

There is a point in my walk around the fields where I go a little further to stare at the wall that marks the easement, that place where our home is not really ours. The wall is old, put together with misshapen stones and loose cement, but refuses to move when I press on it. I wish I could tear it down with my bare hands. I feel as though it serves only to mark my inability to master this place, some monument to my failure here, where the plants and Josh are thriving, and yet I still don't feel at home. I have to force myself to move from the wall, to walk the fields over which we have, at least, some control.

In the fields we have planted all the things that will grow this time of year. We know it won't be much, but hopefully enough to see us through. And we have our last pay cheques, if need be. We are not afraid of autumn or winter. We are prepared, have stockpiled woollens and gloves and tinned soup. The winter isn't true death, anyway. There is always spring – I have always loved spring.

Out in the fields, the tomato stalks grow, roots take hold, cabbages blossom. It is as though we are finally getting a hold of our new lives here. Then it comes, with no sign or omen. It is just there; all around us, endless and suffocating.

I have never known anything like it, not even in high summer in Michigan. The heat passes over the fields, bows the tomato stalks, pulls the sticky green leaves down. We can barely lift our limbs in it. It feels like drowning.

Josh and I lie on the sofa, on each other, taking it in turns to go replenish our water glasses. The whole day is fever. When our skin touches it presses then melts, holds, gives.

'It'll pass,' Josh says. 'It'll be good for the plants. All the heat. Like a hothouse.'

'It should be fall by now,' I say.

'Just hold out. It'll roll over us and out across the Pacific. Then it's all apples and cider and snow. Just think of snow.'

I try to think of snow as I go get two glasses of water. The ice melts before I make it back from the kitchen. Josh gulps his water and then mine too, when I tell him my stomach feels swollen with the heat, that my belly is swollen with this sticky heat and lukewarm water. He says I should go see the doctor if I'm not feeling well. But I'm not feeling unwell; just uncomfortably full, swollen in the heat from my breasts to my toes.

'I'll feel better when the heat passes,' I tell him. 'I just hope it's soon.'

The heat does not give. It persists. It drains the days of colour, turns them nicotine yellow, half seen through glare.

The air conditioner breaks. We cling to the walls and what little cool they give. We live on the couch. Outside the window, the tomato stalks wither. The cabbage blossoms die. The world begins to wilt.

Everything we plant dies. Nothing will rise from the soil. I wait behind the windows while Josh walks up and down the fields, up and down the fields, watering, hosing, installing sprinklers, and all of it useless. The heat takes everything. I feel it move inside me: in my arms and my eyes, under my tongue, in my ears, swelling in my stomach like a long, hot breath. Everything is glass. Everything is so close to breaking. Nothing will rise from the soil.

The sleeplessness of the first night returns. After Josh falls asleep I get up and fetch a glass of water and sit by the window, watching the moon shift over the barren fields. From this point, the night looks cooler than the house, though when I open the window a fraction, the heat crawls in like a cat left out for the day. When I press my fingers to the glass I can almost feel how close the air is out there. It is too much. Is this what I left Michigan for? It had never been my idea to come here, but Josh's.

'I've been thinking about the future,' he had said, as we walked home from dinner at an Italian off Catherine Street. He had his jacket over his arms and as we walked our shoulders touched, drifted, and joined again, as if our bodies were nervous that the other had left.

'How can you be thinking about the future?' I asked. 'It's so perfect tonight. The weather, the food, the walk. Ann Arbor is perfect in spring. I don't want the future, I want this moment to last.'

'It's nice,' he said. 'But you don't want to be here for ever, do you?'

'I've never really thought about it,' I said, honestly.

'I have,' he said.

Instead of taking the turn for our street we walked on and off into another direction. Poplar trees swayed in the evening breeze, and in a playground to the right, a small child swung in a red swing set.

'So what have you been thinking about, Joshua?' I asked. He smiled; he enjoys it when I use his full name.

'About us,' he said. 'And the future.'

'Oh yeah?'

'And it doesn't involve Ann Arbor, or Michigan. It involves some land out west, and growing old, and a couple of kids.'

'And sweet tea?' I asked.

'That's the South,' he said. 'And please, I'm serious.'

He wore a pained expression, as if desperate for me to recognise just how earnest he was about this.

'What do you think?' he asked. 'I think farm life would suit you.'

Is this what he had had in mind? I look out over the fields. The tomato stalks slump sadly, sentinels left on a battlefield they have lost. There is nothing left of the other vegetables but husks. Perhaps a seed remains, in the dirt, stubbornly, but nothing seems to stir.

Josh turns in his sleep behind me. He dreams. He has always dreamed: of this life, of the future. But those dreams have never belonged to me. Just as this house does not belong to me. On paper, at least. Just as the land does not belong to either of us, but is kept, in reserve, for the government. Everything here is someone else's. Nothing here is mine.

Unable to be in the house any longer, I take a glass of water out into the fields. The heat has made me slow and swollen, but it feels good to walk the dry fields. The bare stalks comfort me; there is an honesty to them, in their death, in how they refuse to pretend to thrive here, in this strange place where they find themselves hemmed in by wooden poles and insect nets and stone walls.

Even the easement wall suffers from the heat: its cement has cracked and fissured, the stones sit in it like teeth in worn gums. I reach out for one about the size of my palm, grab it, feel it loosen in my hand and come free with a twist. I shudder; the sheer pleasure of it.

I put the stone in the pocket of my nightdress and take it back to the house with me. I keep my hand on it as I climb into bed and try to fall asleep, feel it close to me, the harsh edges of it. It is mine, this little stone I've torn free. It belongs to me and no one else: it is neither the easement nor the farmland, not the government's or Josh's. It is mine and I cherish it.

I envy the dead stalks their starkness. The heat has worked the opposite in me: I am ballooning by the day, my dresses stick sweat-slick and afford me no modesty. Everything clings and shows where what was once concave is now convex.

My reflection distorts more and more each day. I feel the heat inside my stomach like one long breath. The heat persists. I balloon, day by day, larger among the withered tomato stalks and dried vines where nothing will grow.

I make daily pilgrimages to the wall. Though I leave less and less of it when I leave, the stones seem smaller and smaller in my hands.

Joshua knows nothing about the stones. I complain about stomach upsets and he brings home some Pepto-Bismol, but the lurid pink just makes me nauseous. I have begun being ill on a daily basis, as if my body wishes it could expel the heat that has invaded it, which expands under my skin, until I feel as though I could pop. I cannot bear it much longer.

The death of Josh's mother was the first death in my life. I was unsure what to do with it at first, what I should say to it, do for it. It entered our life as stillness, and dark, and outpourings of grief in unexpected places. Josh's father crying at the gas station while the counter ticked off dollars. Josh crying as he brushed his teeth. The only person who didn't cry was me.

The death touched everything. But Josh was alive. He needed to eat, and drink, and sleep. I made him sandwiches, brewed him coffee, put him to bed when all he would do was sit and read until his eyes were raw. This was how I navigated death: with rhythm, with repetition.

The death did not bring as large a change as I had expected. There was a woman, then she was gone. The changes were all small and scattered. We no longer went over for lunch at the weekend. No one called in the evening. We stopped saying her name. The days went by and closed over the gap – time shut the wound.

The two big changes were: Josh took his mother's books, and I found him looking at properties out west.

Eager to put the death behind us, I said nothing.

Josh has begun spending most of his time in the study. Over the past week, we have barely seen each other. Our affections have turned. Now we hold water glasses to us at all times, as if their bodies, only temporarily cool, could satisfy the thirst that has possessed us.

When I refill my glass I see him in the study, on the floor, books open all around him, poring through marginalia in search of something left of what has gone. I walk from the door before he notices me.

Whether Josh registers my absence or my movements, I am unsure. He seems too possessed with reading through his mother's books; as if the heat has installed some obsession in him, as if he thinks he can find a way beyond its impasse in the pages. I, too, have settled into a new rhythm, a new repetition: stone by stone I take the wall apart, new sections becoming loose the longer the heat persists.

Some stones I keep: ones whose shape pleases me, or feels good to touch through the pockets of whatever I am wearing. By now there are too many to keep, and I don't want to leave them by the wall in case Josh comes and puts them back. I take the stones and move around the fields, leaving small piles of them as I go. Little cairns. When I pile them up I feel as though I am marking something, but just what I'm not sure.

The wall comes undone. The cairns gather all around the fields. And still the heat won't pass, still there is no relief. Josh reads in the study. I build cairns and walk around the house with my pockets full of stones, just waiting to drown in this world without water. How can Josh think of a future like this? Nothing here grows. Everything here feels like death.

Everything quiets, everything that has until then been speaking, imperceptibly – the trees, the bugs, the grass; the floorboards, the piping, the window casements – stills. Is silent. The windows are open but still it comes in: like a breath, blown through. The air lifts, hushes.

I go to the window and press myself against it. For the first time in a long time the glass is cold. Out across the fields, rain plummets. I see the ground darkening from behind the beads of rain on the windowpane.

Something in the air changes. A severity in it lessens. The world is like aloe. The plastic leaves drip blood-black, the tomato stalks sway and soak in the fall, the fissures of earth are filled with rain, melt, join, and close. Everything is mud. Everything is sutured.

I see Josh run into the rain. He runs out among the tomato stalks. He holds his hands up to the air and spins in the rain. The rain welcomes him. It washes him clean. His feet sink into the mud. His hair sticks to his forehead. He stands hands outstretched, mouth open, drinking it in. All around him my stones welcome the rain.

Josh doesn't even see them, these little stones that mark how far we have come, what has passed.

I smile at the window, watching the rain make the old cement of the wall slick again, watch what is left of it begin to slide, unable to bear the weight of all this water on it. The barrier cannot hold in this new world of rain, cool and calm and new. The wall collapses. Joshua spins in the rain. In the downpour, my cairns look like flowerbeds. As if I have planted something in them that will spring to life.

With the wall gone, neither Josh nor the government can tell whose his whose. The land is just land. There are no walls or tracks to mark it anyone's. Except for a couple of stones, piled here and there around the property. In the future, perhaps, someone will come and find them, imagine what purpose they served, to whom they belonged. What kind of person raised these wordless monuments. Maybe they will check the documents, find ownership records for the house in Josh's name, documents on which my name doesn't appear; not even in a margin or a footnote. No one will know that they belonged to me, and their future, too, is mine. But the future has never interested me. It is Josh who dreams of the future. Josh, who now wheels open-armed in the fields he doesn't quite own, drinking in the rain.

I go from the window, downstairs. The rooms are cool now, quiet. In the kitchen I make two sandwiches, wrap one in cling film and leave it on the table, brew the French press, set out two cups and pour myself one with a splash of milk and two sugars. Absent-mindedly I pile sugar cubes while I sip my coffee, forming a little pyramid in the middle of the table. When Josh comes in from the rain he sits down to eat his sandwich and drink. It feels as if it's the first time we've seen each other in years.

'It's over,' he says, smiling through a mouth full of sandwich. He looks at the sugar on the table, puzzled. I place the final cube on the pyramid. 'The heat's left.'

It does feel as if something has left, some menace in the air. It is hard to recall what it felt like to be in that fever; it seems so far away. Another world. But the heat has not left. Not entirely. My belly is still swollen – my fingers, my toes, my breasts. It stirs in me like something living.

'I think we need to talk,' I tell him. 'About the future.'

The Call

Up the mountain. Through birch bones. Through leaf-whispers. Away from camp, where the children should be rising, bleary, pre-dawn, putting on orange T-shirts. 'Camp Wolfcreek' in stylised timber font above a black wolfprint. Adam Green swipes tree branches as he ascends. Leaves, full and summer-green, settle in his hair. He shakes his head and they scatter.

He should be there. Should be making sure they brush their teeth, comb their hair, get to breakfast on time. He should be shouting names: Harley, Katy, Gwenn, Chris, Crystal. *Rise and shine.* And they would be looking at him the whole time, oddly wise, like little sages, perceiving in his accent a certain oddness, an out-of-placeness that is more than his Galway whiteness. He thinks to himself that, yes, that is what he should be doing, that is what he is, after all, being paid to do. But he does not turn back. There is nothing to go back for.

You can't run away from this, son.

The trees diminish as he rises; the air becomes thinner. He climbs steps on the winding path, legs stretching up ridges formed by root-snarls. The ground dips suddenly, the forest spilling out on to a tarn: all round the lake steep peaks rise and, in the water's surface, quiver, snow clinging still to the peaks despite the summer sun, now beginning its ascent on the far shore. Where the sun touches it, the water is brilliant aquamarine. The wind brings waves in skeins of arrowheads toward him.

You can't run away from this, son.

His mother's voice speaks from his phone. The plastic is warm against his ear, the screen clouded with skin flakes. He hits the repeat button and sits on the lake shore, on a bed of pebbles that glitter cold in the morning light.

You can't run away from this, son.

It is the 'son'; it digs under his skin. As if he has forgotten, as if his flight across the ocean, his six-week seclusion, amounts to a total abandonment of filial duty.

Doesn't it? Hadn't that, after all, been the point?

You can't run away from this, son.

Adam stands. The pebbles cling to him in a pattern reminiscent of chain mail. He takes the phone in his hand, hits the playback button. His mother begins to speak. He launches the phone in one clear arc.

You can't run—

The phone drops into aquamarine. The arrows of the waves shatter. Silence, invisibly expansive, stills the small noises of the woods, mountains, lake: the leaf-shake, the water-hush, the fox-paw scratch. The to and fro of voles and moles and larks. For a moment, for one brief shiver, everything – everything ceases.

Something emerges from the lake. A blade, a hilt, a sword in a milk-white hand, undoubtedly female. The hand gleams as if covered in gold scales.

All he has to do is take it. All he has to do is put his hand out. The sword will be there, he knows it. It will move invisibly from the lake to his hand, so fast the water of the lake will be unruffled. And something will have been decided.

He can see it, see himself – clearly, as if he has stepped outside himself briefly – on the lakeshore with the sword held high, morning light fierce along its edge. He seems strong, capable. He will go forth in pursuit of – here the vision is indistinct, an outline of an image, the ghost of a girl, the suggestion of a crown. When he has the sword he will know what to do, know what he will get in return for carrying it. There is a bargain being struck here. He is being offered strength and promise and being more than mortal.

— *away from this, son*.

It begins with a ring. A silver band in a radish patch, sapphire the size of a thumbnail, glowing. The tilled earth in the grave-light is that of another world, one far removed from Galway, the farm, the parochial life eight-year-old Adam Green is living. He stares at the ring, radishes in hand. Odd sigils are carved along the band.

'What ye got there, now?' his father asks, wiping his hands with a rag.

Adam doesn't touch the ring. His father comes and looks at it. He moves to touch it and arcs of electric blue crackle along his hand. The air smells of burning hair. Adam can taste the smoke on his tongue as he helps his father into the house.

That night, they – his father, his mother, and him – go to look for the ring in the allotment behind the house. They dig in the dirt, but nothing comes forward, save a few gnarled radishes, an earthworm, and several small stones that look like teeth.

They never speak of it again, but Adam knows: that only he could have touched that ring. It had been meant for him. He stops helping his father pull the vegetables out of the garden. He thinks his father might take issue with it, but he accepts it, as if he had expected it all along. As if he knows why Adam is afraid to put his hands in the dirt.

Adam's mum picks him up from primary school. She parks the car in front of the church across the road and waits. Adam crosses with the lollipop man, every day, without fail, like a good boy should, though at ten years old he is pretty sure he can cross the road by himself. Nevertheless, he waits with the kind old man in the yellow jacket until he says it is time to cross as he steps into the road with his staff held high and brings the cars to a halt.

There is a younger boy with him today. He walks behind Adam as he crosses the road, the lollipop man smiling at them both as they pass. The lollipop man walks back to the other side. The boy behind Adam stops to tie his shoelaces in the middle of the road.

And Adam feels it. All he has to do is grab the lad, draw him across the tarmac to the kerbside, as a car shoots past with a sound like wings buffeting. It will be a different sort of valour. It will not involve rings or lightning. But a bargain, nonetheless. And from there on out, he will never accomplish anything more.

Adam stands and stares as the boy ties his shoelaces. First the left lace of his left shoe, over the right lace, round, under, loop. Adam sees something moving out of the corner of his eye. He remains motionless, devoted to this moment of indecision. He refuses. He refuses to step forth. Metal screams in the air.

When Adam is sixteen, he is desperately in love with Clara McDougal. She is everything. She is dark hair, green eyes, impossible legs. She smells of apples and pencil shavings and every time he passes her in school odd muscles in his stomach levitate. He thinks about her in English, in Irish, in mathematics, conjuring her form in a series of adjectives and shapes: rhomboid, *meallacach*, *foirfe*, heart-faced (two semi-circles, one triangle [isosceles]), perfection. The teacher drones on, buzzing, a bee at the open window by which she sits, taking notes. He gets so lost in his head, in the idea of her, that he doesn't see her vanish.

One minute she is there, the next she is gone. On her desk is a folded-up square of paper sealed with blue wax. The window is open. He hasn't imagined that part. She is gone through the window and no one has noticed except him.

And he knows: if he reads the letter, it will be decided. He will go forth. There will be a fortress, in the woods, a house (possibly edible), a woman, a man, a black robe, a curse, jealousy. These parts are undecided. They are in motion. It all depends on his stepping out, into this other world beyond the window. He must leave school behind, his family behind – he must relinquish all claim to banality. This is the trade. The bargain. The pact.

His father is diagnosed when Adam is twenty-one. His mother tells him nothing for weeks, while his father becomes secretive, forever popping out and coming back ashen. When they can no longer hide it they tell Adam his father is dying.

But you can save him, his mother says.

His father cannot look at him. He knows, that this is so much to ask, that he is putting everything on his son. And he must. But he cannot. He looks at the wall while his wife speaks.

The operation is safe, she says. *Your life would be the same afterwards, it would be OK, it would all be OK. It's just a little piece of you. Just a little sacrifice.*

You could be a hero, she says. *Please. Be a hero.*

Adam Green takes his father's credit card and goes to Dublin. At an internet cafe on Grafton Street, near the statue of Molly Malone, he finds a summer job in Wyoming. He gets on a plane and leaves behind: a ring, a letter, a farm outside Galway.

And his mother leaves a message on the voicemail on his phone.

You can't run away from this, son.

There is something about the children at the camp, how life is laid out before them, undecided. They are still growing into themselves, still tumble awkwardly over their own feet as they run pell-mell alongside the wood cabins. They laugh freer, unabashedly joyous. It seems easier to breathe when they are near. Adam begins to think he has made the right decision, though at night he presses his phone to his ear and listens to his mother speak. He has no signal on the phone, no credit left, but it holds the last fragment of something he cannot fully give up. He is almost positive he has made the right decision, but when his mother speaks he is not so sure.

Weeks pass. The camp will only last for six, with children in variations, out of their parents' hair for a brief time across June and August. Adam teaches them how to light a campfire, how to sing around it (he tries to teach them 'Óró sé do bheatha 'bhaile' but they all want to sing something about a man called John Jacob Jingleheimer Schmidt).

They push him. They rebel, rage, scream, cry, run, return. They push and test and tear at limits. And his response to them is measured, calm, controlled. When he does this he feels more human than some figure with a sword, stuck in a suit of armour, off to take a girl in his arms as if she has no legs. He feels himself becoming himself. A man refusing both gifts and bravery, refusing to be bound. A man. No more, no less.

Adam wakes in the night. He feels the weight of another person in the room, but when he turns the light on he is alone. He hears noise through the door that connects to the children's bunks, but it seems far away, muffled by whatever fog still lies in his mind. He tries to shake his head clear, but still it feels like a ball of cotton wool: bunched up, indistinct. He turns over to try and get back to sleep, but the sheets are soaked; his legs slip over each other, greased with sweat. It is too hot. That sound from the other room. Like a faint calliope. It is too hot. And what is that smell? A raw, animal scent on the bed sheets, and something charred. The dark burn of charcoal. But the fire had been put out before bed. Hadn't it?

Adam sits bolt upright and looks at the door. Smoke coils beneath it, conspires along the ceiling. The children are burning. Too tired, too beaten by the heat to scream properly. The whimper on the other side of the door. Waiting.

He feels it: this moment of decision, to step forward, to be what he is meant to be. He must give up normality, must put the needs of the world before his own. He has been feeling like a man all this time but now that it comes down to it, to this moment of gritted teeth and jaw held high, he is not sure he can bring himself to do it.

And if he does? The children will worship him, will behave, will do whatever he wants. Their parents will embrace him, will whisper 'thank you's on his shoulder. They will call him a hero. And he will have to give it up. Give up everything to become it. No more human failings, human vices, human passions – a hero. This and nothing more. All he has to do is go through the door; all he has to do is answer the call.

The hand holds the sword in the water. Whose hand is it? What body moves behind these gestures, these deaths, these calamities? Who is calling?

Adam is distrustful. He has seen too much sacrifice, too many heroes made and made to vanish: Conchobar mac Nessa; Fionn mac Cumhaill; Gráinne Mhaol; the Fianna; Brian Boru; Patrick Pearse; Michael Collins; Éamon de Valera. Bobby Sands, Patsy O'Hara, Michael Devine. And what is their legacy? What is left of them but the name, the head lopped off, the walls of their prison cells still stained with excreta? Is this the price of immortality?

He will not pay for something he has never wanted. He did not want it in a radish patch, did not want it with vanishing Clara, did not want it when his father would not ask. He did not want it as the cabin collapsed. Did not want it in the searing air or the needling heat. And he does not want it now, by this lake, on this mountain. He wants life, not legend.

But what is left for him now? He knows his mother will

never forgive him, and he doesn't even know if his father is still alive. The camp. The children. Those he should have protected. He has gained nothing for it. For all the things he has lost trying not to lose himself. But this sword, like a compass needle, keeps swinging back to this same decision, time and time again, inevitable as north, awaiting the time when he will finally say yes. And he knows, one day, he will have to answer the call. That the game is rigged from the start. That the dealer always wins.

The lake water rises to meet him. He steps into it. The hand trembles slightly, but never loses grip of the sword. It has waited so long for this. A few seconds more. He walks toward it, legs unsettling silt. The bottom of the lake remains level. It is part of the hand's magic, he is sure. It is bending the world to it. To this trade, this becoming of the figure of a man.

The sword is there. In that hand, which is, up close, almost transparent. All he has to do is reach out and take it. He will be great. He will be forgiven his indiscretions, his vehicular negligence, his wilful manslaughter. Because he will no longer be Adam Green, once farmer, prodigal son, lustful teenager. He will be something more than a man, and something less. He reaches out. The blade glitters, keen. Somewhere in the wood, a lone bird raises its call. There is no one there to answer.

The Ends of the Earth

It's almost silly how painful it is. To wake up and feel a chill in the bed where he should be. To make more coffee than needed and drink it anyway. To sit at a breakfast bar, hands jittering, with no one to talk to. To turn at the door, cheek ready, for a kiss that won't come. The skin there seems colder as Alan walks to work, braced against the December air. Ross would have told him that that's not how it works. That cells have no memory. And he knows that – but he feels it anyway.

All day at work he sets copy, adjusts margins, unscrambles text. Distractedly. On his lunch break he sends a text to Angus, arranging to meet later. A welcome break; he is less lonely after the exchange. *The usual place, after work, might be late.* And as he sits in the pub waiting for him to get there, messages fly, telling him how close he is. Right now that's all he wants. That's all he needs: someone close.

'How you doing?' Angus asks, elbows on the graffitied table, face hollowed by the dim light bulbs.

He shrugs. Angus nods, as though an entire conversation has passed.

'You'll be fine, you always are. It's not like it's a surprise.

He does this every year.'

'I know,' he says. 'But...'

'But what?'

'It's embarrassing.'

'At this point, what could be embarrassing?'

Angus is right. He knows everything. Everything that happened in the heady nights of their twenties. He remembers the quiet conversations on Sundays in this same pub, extinguished, drinking just for restoration. He knows all about the men before Ross, and the women; the people Alan would rather forget. All the failure; Angus knows it. The secret history. The other biography.

'Well,' he says. 'Since they passed that law...'

'Oh,' Angus says. 'You guys are thinking about getting married?'

'I don't know,' he says, shaking his head. 'Ross has just been weird.'

'You think he's going to propose?'

'I thought so. We went out for a meal the day before he left. That place in the West End, with the mezzanine and the skylight. Stars shining, candlelight, a bottle of champagne. I don't know. He was distracted, like he was thinking about something important. I thought he was going to ask.'

'And?'

'Nothing.'

'And you're upset he didn't?'

'No, no. It's not that. Something just feels different. Like... we're distant.'

'You are,' Angus says. 'For a bit, anyway. But distance isn't all it used to be. Just give him a call, you'll feel better.'

When he gets back to the empty house, the cold air in his lungs as he climbs the three flights of the Battlefield close, he sits down on the couch with a cup of tea and a book. *The Snow Geese*. William Fiennes. He thought it would be nice for them to read together while he was away. Make them closer. A little bit of both their jobs: books and birds. Flight and flight of fancy.

He put a copy of the same book in brown wrapping and snuck it on the ship with Ross. As he opens the first page, pressing the fresh paper which flutters as it wakes, he imagines him, on a boat on the southernmost sea. His fingers on the same pages. The same journey; start to finish. Together. All the way to the end.

*

'You get used to it,' he says. 'It's just your mind misunderstanding distance.'

Somebody vomits over the side of the ship.

'Try looking at the ones in flight; it'll help.'

Gratifying *ah*'s as the birds swoop and soar. He flexes his right hand to disperse the chill that has settled there.

'Look at that one,' a woman says. 'It flies like a bat.'

'It's a petrel,' he says, without looking; he knows by now how the passengers take to them, the birds out here not filled with the elegance they expect.

'Wilson's storm petrel, I think,' says another woman. There's always one.

It's not just the money that does it. He would never have understood that, back home, home-home, if it's even still that. This kind of life – his now, as well, he supposes – was unimaginable to him there, then, when the close-knittedness of small-town life had him on edge. He supposes that's why he likes these tours so much: the open air.

He had thought money, particularly this vintage, made people insufferable. He supposes it came from those little remarks people made – without thinking – about the smallness of places, their remove from the world, and how desperate it would be to live there. All of university had been like that. When he left, for the first time. How far has he come? Would he recognise himself, if he met him now, that little boy in Canada, or that younger man, scraping by to get through a doctorate?

It isn't money that makes the people on the ship the way they are; it's the hobby. It breeds a sort of genteel competitiveness. He wonders if they notice, how their comments come to mime the birds: a delicate correction soars across the bow, the retort a flutter of wings.

'Still, though. It's really quite beautiful,' someone says.

He supposes it is, at that.

After the observation, he goes to his quarters below deck. He should have been taking notes, writing down talking points for the lecture the following afternoon, but still that sharp bite in his hand, like gripping a snowball. Cold, needling.

There is a knock at the door. One of the administrative gofers.

'Sorry to interrupt you, sir,' the boy says. He resents the 'sir'. The boy's cheeks are flush, his eyes bright. Not a day above twenty-four. He resents this, too; the pink cheeks, the sharpness of the eyes. 'But there was a parcel for you with some of the cargo.'

'A parcel?' he asks, taking the package from the boy's hands. Brown paper expertly folded around a light oblong. As it passes between them, their fingers touch, briefly. There again, that needling pain.

He ignores it as he closes the door and sits down at the desk bolted to the wall. There is a card on the parcel, familiar handwriting, and a simple inscription: *Überraschung! Kiss*.

How long had it been since Berlin? Thirteen years now, it must be. And still he remembers the candlelight, sharp shards of it glittering in a pair of green eyes in a strange apartment, and a birthday cake drifting from somewhere in the ether. A toy motorcycle in the icing, the number eight on its headlight. And the word: *Überraschung!*

He puts the package down unopened and begins getting ready for the evening meal. The buttons of his dinner jacket are impossible; the fingers of his right hand refuse to grasp the faux-pearl finish. He sits down on the end of the bed and twists the thick ring on his middle finger, trying his best not to look at the parcel on the desk, which sits there, almost accusingly.

*

A week gone by and still no word. He imagines a boat, capsized, checks his phone and e-mail obsessively, worried he might have to identify a body. One he knew in life, intimately, most intimately. Would he know it in death? Would he recognise him, after the sea change a drowning works on the body? But then he realises that they would phone Ross's father in Canada first. Would he even call him?

And then again, that worry. That maybe everything is fine. That Ross just doesn't want to talk to him. That enough is enough, that there is nothing new to explore. No life, no adventure, in this city or another. Not with Alan, anyway. But maybe with someone else. He feels a knot in the pit of his stomach: disgust that he almost wishes for a body, something he can hold on to, at the end.

The landline is quiet without Ross. Alan never uses it. But over the week, two messages appear from the doctor, asking Ross to call her back.

'Maybe he's just busy,' Angus says over dinner, dutifully keeping him company in the Battlefield flat.

'Maybe,' he says. 'But something's wrong. I feel it. I know, it's stupid. But I do. I feel it in my guts.'

'You sure that's not just the food?' Angus says.

Even this can't lighten the mood.

'Let's open another bottle of wine,' he says.

'Don't you have work in the morning?' Angus asks.

'Don't you?' he replies.

'Fair point.'

When Angus leaves he fetches his copy of *The Snow Geese* from the living room and takes it to bed. His head swims in Malbec. The words on the page drift. He tries to keep them steady with his finger, tries to press the pages down so they stay still. He thinks of Ross, in the Antarctic, fingers on these same words, following that same journey with the geese, northward, to Baffin Island, to Canada. For a minute he wonders if Ross still thinks of it as home. Home-home. If maybe this flat in Battlefield, this little country filled with rain, him – if all this isn't, and never had been, home.

*

The first turns on board had had a thin, trembling signal; barely enough for a text. Then the next, basic internet, the occasional e-mail fired off between appointments. And now: full access, high speed, video calls. As if he is not there, at the southernmost point; as if he is back in the apartment in Battlefield. And he could be, at that. All it would take is a couple of words, a little interfacing – distance means so little these days.

And yet he finds himself unwilling to call, and ignoring the calls that come through. A week has passed and still no contact. The parcel remains unopened on his desk.

He knows what's inside. It drives Alan mad, but he's always been that way, wanting to see inside things. Even as a kid, he went looking for presents in his mother's wardrobe, when she had still been there, and in the loft when it was just him and his dad. When his father remarried, his stepmom hid the presents in the airing cupboard. And to mark the ages of Mom, Dad, and Stepmom, another type of wrapping: meticulous, all-thumbs, store-bought. Every year, every birthday, every Christmas. Packages held to his ear, then shaken; or to the light to try and see inside. He likes to solve mysteries, to know. Which is why Alan has never let him live down that birthday party in Berlin, where Alan had Ross's friends fly out and meet them, at a friend of a friend of a friend's, who had offered, quite innocently (or so it had seemed), to have them over for a party while they were in the city for the weekend. And then, as he went to put their coats in a bedroom, all those familiar faces shouting: *Überraschung!*

He learned no German on the trip, or any of the ones after, but he holds that word very close to him. Even now, instead of the word 'surprise' he often finds himself thinking *Überraschung.*

He knows what lies there on the desk, though Alan has wrapped it in two layers of brown paper to hide the title. He remembers a conversation a week before he left, in the kitchen, drinking coffee, legs touching idly at the breakfast

bar, talking into cereal bowls and mugs shaped like swans –
a tasteless gift from one of his stepsisters – where the neck
formed the handle. And Alan had been so excited, talking
about this book he found, about birds.

'But not really *about* birds, you know?' he said. 'It's about
a man who's obsessed with them because he's been conva-
lescing. And the birds represent something for him. Freedom
or something. Home. I don't know, but it sounds good.'

He had nodded, smiling, half listening; familiar with the
enthusiasm.

He sits on the edge of the bed staring at the parcel,
twisting his father's wedding ring on the middle finger of
his right hand. And the missed calls pile up. Notifications on
his computer he can't bring himself to look at. If he answers
the phone, he knows, he will have to have the conversation.

This trip is all numbness: in his hand, in his chest. But
still, he cannot bring himself to unwrap the parcel on the
desk, or trace the words on those pages. They are part of
another journey. And no phone call will change how far he
feels from the path those words take. He is not there; he
is here. Alone, on this boat, at the southern tip, where life
barely holds. Here, at the ends of the earth.

*

It's his job: he moves words, sets them, adjusts their margins.
His job is to determine just how they will look on the page.
Not a writer, not that, no. But he has always felt close to
words. A closeness in them. As if they bring him closer to the
person behind them. This is why he reads. To feel someone
else's thoughts, close to his own. It's why he's kept all the
letters, from a time when letters were currency instead of

trash. All the little communications between him and Ross, even the occasional postcard from Angus. Shoeboxes in the cupboard. A thick sheaf marked by postage stamps, customs seals, held together by a strained elastic band. Sometimes he pulls them out to read them; to feel the thoughts of a younger man, a younger him. He doesn't recognise the person who wrote those letters. But he remembers the Ross who wrote his. Young Canadian, determined to succeed, determined to map the evolution of birds, the perfection of their hollow bones.

If only they were birds, he thinks. They always come back. Isn't that what migration is all about? For the first time in their relationship, he wishes he knew what Ross knows about them. The mechanism that guides them home. But he is not Ross. He doesn't have science, or the safety of knowing how these things work. All he has is words.

Stubbornly, he continues to send them flying to the southern sea. And of those he sets loose, not one returns.

*

He will be home in a few days. And still, the parcel is unopened, the calls unanswered. At this point, it has gone on so long, he is afraid to break the silence. It feels as though he would be giving something up.

He distracts himself with the final lectures, final observation sessions, final PowerPoint presentations. Everything is final, now, he supposes. He tries to savour it: the monotony of the repetition, these words he knows by heart, these slides, even the chill in his hand, the needling in his nerves. He tries to feel it: everything, while he still can.

The needles are moving up his wrist as he makes the last

PowerPoint. At this point, he is using mainly his left hand to move the photographs he's taken, the brief explanations, the Latin terms that remind the passengers of childhoods in good schools and stern men conjuring dead tongues. Notifications fire up on the screen. Numbers stare at him, demanding attention, a response. An email appears on the screen from Alan, the message: *Doctor called. Everything OK? Please call back.*

He ignores the email and finishes the PowerPoint. Unable to work the delicate buttons of his dinner jacket, he goes to dine in a bare shirt.

At dinner he drinks more port than he should, but his boss doesn't care, and the passengers enjoy seeing him let go, now the trip is almost over. Do you have a girlfriend? they ask him. A handsome man like you, I'm sure you do well with the ladies. I bet she's missing you dreadfully. But you have all these gadgets these days, I'm sure you talk all the time. Not like in our day. Love letters, by hand you know. Used to make the fingers cramp something awful.

'I've got someone at home,' he says. The wedding band worries a line in his finger.

'Not married yet? Very modern, I suppose. Still, though, about time you made an honest woman of her.'

Outside the ship's windows the ice floes melt in the Antarctic summer. The birds wheel in the sky: some flying deftly, while others are ungainly, like bats, fluttering through the air. Everyone thinks of flight when they think of birds; of flight patterns, thermal upheaval and migration, the delicacy of their bones.

But there is not a single bird that does not nest; all this soaring is part of that search. They are trying to find some safe place to land. Even here, where the ice is melting; where home is vanishing before their eyes.

*

He starts preparing for him coming home. Not a word the entire two and a half weeks. And so he prepares twice. He does what he normally would: buys venison from the butcher and a six-pack of stout. He washes the sheets, hangs them out to dry. He cleans the flat, mechanically. And he prepares for disaster: packs a bag of clothes, mentally works through what it would take to separate, tries not to feel the pain as he realises the only thing they share together, legally, is the mortgage on the flat. Symbolic, more than anything else. Ross makes the mortgage payments. When Ross gets back, when he tells him not only does he not want to marry him, but their life together is coming to an end, there will be nothing left.

Once he has exhausted all the little tasks, he writes a note on the pad next to the machine: *Doctor called again. Says it's important. Are you OK?*

The pen holds for a moment over the pad; his hand shakes. As though he wants to write something else, but isn't quite sure what. Unable to capture the words on the tip of his tongue, he instead writes underneath the first lines: *Welcome home.*

*

It's ending, the reprieve. These two and a half weeks he's had from everything. Just the birds, the ice floes, these old people from older money who pay too much for an educational vacation. These old people he would have hated, once upon a time, but who like him, who think he's someone he's

119

not. Someone he almost wants to be.

The parcel lies on his desk, unopened. Ross twists his father's wedding ring on his finger as he stares at it.

He had known it was coming, or that it might. He isn't quite sure. A part of him knew, at least. He has shot down enough birds, opened them up and seen inside, to know that genetics keeps its share of secrets, but that sometimes it is clear about what it will give – no illusions, just cells, mutation. A process of evolution in one direction or the other. He had known, but he didn't want to believe.

When he met Alan all those years ago, he had been sure that that was it, that that was the rest of his life – him. And sixteen years. Sixteen years of life, of love, of things being, not perfect, but not far from it, either. And now in the year they can finally marry, this year of his forty-second birthday, it comes to an end. He had managed, by some miracle, to be asymptomatic, to have avoided, apparently, the slow death that had taken his mother. He had grown complacent. He had let himself hope. And then that numbness, and the pinched pain in his fingertip, the one on which he wears his father's first wedding ring, the one he thought he would wear when he married, the one he kept, for that occasion, the one he was going to give to Alan, before he left, in that restaurant they went to on Ashton Lane, with the stars above them, and the champagne, fizzing. But he had seen the doctor that morning, for the results of a check-up. Just routine, before every trip, but then she had said those words: *I have bad news.* And how could he?

How do you say that? How do you tell someone you can't, after all this, all these years and all this waiting, all these struggles and legislation, that you can't, in the end?

He finishes packing. The ship will dock in a few hours.

He is going home; whatever that means.

*

'So what are you going to do?' Angus says.

'I don't know,' he says. 'I don't know what I'd say. It feels like I've been letting him go; getting ready for the hit, bracing for a punch. And now he might be back. I don't know whether to be happy or sad. A part's been letting go and another's been holding on, hoping. Imagining him walking through the door with a smile, and some excuse that makes me feel stupid for even doubting it. I try and read and my eyes can't focus on the page. Every time I try I just feel sick. Like carsick, or seasick.'

'Is he back in the country yet?'

'His flight got in an hour ago.'

'So he's probably home by now?'

'Probably.'

They remain silent for a moment; the only sound is Angus's partner Gillian, pottering about their flat, pointedly silent. He knows he shouldn't be here, unannounced. He is taking up too much of Angus's time. But he needs him. Needs someone close to him.

'So,' Angus says, taking a quick glug of beer. 'What are you going to do?'

*

He kicks his shoes off at the door and lets them lie, the way he does when they come back from a night out, and throws his keys in the dish, hears that familiar chime. He doesn't call out. He simply walks into the living room and its open-plan kitchen, expecting to see him there, curled on the couch with *Snow Geese* in his hands and a glass of Malbec, maybe even asleep. He imagines leaning down over the edge of the sofa and waking him with a kiss.

The flat is empty. Empty, but warm. The oven on and two plates inside covered in tin foil. Alan is not home.

He sits on the couch and, for the first time since returning, feels on solid ground. There is a book in the left corner, wedged between the arm and the cushion. *The Snow Geese.* A train ticket bookmark, Toronto to Windsor, marks his place in the book. That bookmark Alan had kept since they visited Ross's family out in Windsor, had had an awkward dinner with his grandmother, who spoke to Alan in that accent she had never lost since leaving Ayrshire.

He goes to the fridge and looks inside. Sure enough, a six-pack of stout, just for him. He opens a bottle and stands in the kitchen, smelling that smell, the smell of home that is insensible until a return, more vivid now he has spent so much time in the clear blast of the southern winds and the stuffy quarters below deck.

He goes to his bag and takes out the parcel and sits down on the couch. This is the longest he has ever gone without opening a present; a weakness Alan calls the only thing that proves he had ever been a child. He supposes it is childish, at that, to be so concerned with gifts. But his mother always made a big deal about them; made them by hand because they didn't have enough money. And he likes to keep that – her, at least some part. He still remembers how his father twisted his wedding ring nervously, sitting on the narrow bed and saying he was sorry, but at least she wasn't in pain any more. It had been the day before his tenth birthday.

When they went through his mother's things a year

later, they found a package, wrapped in paper printed with rockets. An old T-shirt on which she had embroidered a kestrel and his name.

He still has it, somewhere, somewhere in the cupboard next to those shoeboxes of old letters Alan keeps. He will have to pack it when he leaves. As he sits there, in his new home, this new life he can no longer keep, he is almost happy to know that his mother has managed to give him one last gift. Even if he has to leave everything else behind, he supposes he will have that, at least, in the end.

*

He takes the train back from Angus's flat. But instead of walking to Central Station from Queen Street, he idles in George Square. He walks by the ice rink, the fair, the chairs spinning in the clean winter air. Between the couples, whispering, cold noses on numb cheeks, kissing with chapped lips. He makes his way to the Gallery of Modern Art and sits on the steps in front of the Christmas trees. The fairy lights strung across Merchant Square make the early dark glow. How long till Christmas? He has lost track of days; only the countdown, the return, the time-stamps on all those phone calls. And now he is here, in this time beyond the clock. He doesn't know what to do.

He watches the people go by. Their arms laden with bags, gift-wrap peeking out from the top. Gold bows and red paper, crêpe, the occasionally gaudy star. Some so strongly perfumed he can smell them. He still has to buy Ross a Christmas present. He's so bad with them, always trying to guess. It's tradition now for Alan to hide presents with Angus and go over on the 23rd. They wrap gifts together, drink mulled wine, and let the obligatory *It's a Wonderful Life* play in the background.

Will he even have to buy a present this year? And the New Year. His birthday on the 7th. He realises that he might be starting the new year alone. That at the bells on Hogmanay he might be letting go of these past sixteen years and all they have shared. What is he supposed to do?

But does every man feel like this at forty—

The words rise from somewhere inside him. Somewhere that hasn't quite forgotten his time at school. They are the start of a poem, but he can't remember the poet. He will look it up when he goes home. Look it up, open a bottle of wine, sit on the couch. Finish his book. He can decide on that, at least. Small steps. Deep breaths.

He walks to the train station, cutting across Sauchiehall Street. As he gets the train to Mount Florida, he thinks to himself: is this how every man feels at forty? But he isn't forty. Not quite yet. Not quite at the end. And not quite at a beginning either.

*

He unwraps the parcel, using his left hand, mainly, to tear the two layers of paper. A book slips out: a pale-blue cover, white geese in flight. He puts it to the side.

Into the scraps of paper left, he slips his father's wedding ring, and wraps it, as best he can, sealing it with the rag end of a piece of tape from the original wrapping. He finds a pen and a piece of paper and tries to write down what he has to say: that he is sorry, that he has to tell him something, that he doesn't want to go, but he doesn't want to make him watch. But his right hand refuses to comply, and the left will make only scratches.

Giving up, he leaves the scrawled paper on the table, next to the parcel. His father's wedding ring, from his first marriage, to Ross's mother. He wants Alan to have it, regardless of what's to come. He wanted it to be different; wanted to give it to him in a different way, but now, now that it is happening, this slow death, he wants him to have it, anyway. Maybe it will mean something: even if he can't write the words, even if he can't bring himself to say them.

He takes his copy of the book, opens it up and begins, following the words on the page, from illness to a journey, northbound, to Canada. Back home, for him, if it even is still that. He doesn't know how long he can stay, in this flat, this place that has become home. But he knows he won't be able to make himself leave if he stays much longer. And yet he can't stop himself; he finds himself forgetting, losing himself in the words on the page, the flight of the geese. The fight for home.

He forces himself to close the book, lays it down still open on the table, and stands up to leave. Something catches his eye. Next to the phone, a few words scrawled on a scrap of paper. A message. And two simple words.

The door opens. Alan is standing there, staring at him, keys in his hand, the door still open, his mouth ajar, lips moving slightly, as if searching for the right words, as if there could be any. Ross doesn't know what to say either.

At a loss, he ventures, '*Überraschung.*'

Alan seems hurt, at first. Then something else. He looks at the package on the table, the open bottle of beer. The books. His expression is utterly unreadable.

'Welcome home,' he says, and closes the door.

Between Tongues

Gorm. Pallavi's voice lifted the Gaelic roughly, picked the vowels up by the ears, held tight to the clusters – *chd, bh, mh.* It put the language to work. To say that her accent was 'Indian' didn't really do it justice. When we met that first morning, for our Gaelic class at the library in Stornoway, she told me she grew up with Bengali, English, and Hindi in Calcutta before her family moved to Greenock in the sixties. Pallavi spoke English with a distinctly Scottish flavour, but her Gaelic was something else entirely.

'It's funny,' Pallavi said. 'In Bengali, *gorm* means *hot*. Which isn't what I think of when I think of *blue*. But then, *gorm* in Gaelic also means the colour of grass. So it makes me think of *barsha*, the monsoon season, when the rain keeps down the dust and the flowers grow. It kinda makes sense, when you think about it. Who'd have thought you could think Gaelic in Bengali?'

Gorm. The word teetered in the air, unsure where to find its footing. Above her head, beads of water gathered in the ceiling tiles, dripped, dripped, formed stalactites of glass, before breaking. A maddening flush. A sudden monsoon in a Stornoway classroom. It soaked Pallavi's hair, the jotters on the desks, the list of colours the teacher had written on the whiteboard bled red, yellow, blue. *Dearag, buidhe, gorm.* The vermillion of Pallavi's bindi was beaded with rain. And yet none of the students turned to look. Pallavi herself was unconcerned by the water soaking through the pistachio and gold of her sari, and the gulmohar leaves in the deluge, lotus blooms drifting sedately in the downpour. Droplets of rain on thick leaves, palm, pandan, lush and lifeful. The smell of cinnamon, clove, and rain. The class went on, regardless, as if this kind of transformation were an everyday occurrence.

I looked at my notebook with a strange sense of shame, as if I had seen something I shouldn't have. My notebook was split in two, Gaelic and English, and each page soaked by the rain. Yet in their pliancy they seemed somehow more ready to take in new words. I saw, in gently diffusing ink: *Tha mi sgìth. I am tired.* And under it, a phrase I was still trying to learn: *Tha mi sgìth de bhith air an earalachadh dè dh'fhaodadh is dè nach fhaodadh mi a dhèanamh.*

The lush rain continued to fall, continues to fall, every time I say the word *gorm*. Who would have thought you could think Gaelic in Bengali? Not me. Not then. I was still trying to learn the sentence: *I am sick and tired of being told what I can and cannot do.*

*

In a two-bedroom house on the outside of Stornoway, Ruaraidh and I passed words back and forth. It was not a conversation. To him the words were meaningful, living; to me they were barely animate. I repeated the things I learned in class. I wore my name *on me, orm,* the way love is placed

128

on someone: *mo ghaol ort, my love is on you. 'S e Carrie an t-ainm a th' orm, Carrie is the name on me.* In class the day before, we had learned to talk about professions, which in Gaelic are always *in us.* In the case of one student, a translator between Spanish and English, the teacher said: *'S e eadar-thangair a th' annam. I have a between-tonguer in me.* The word *translation* in Gaelic means: *being between tongues.*

'So what would I say?' I asked Ruaraidh. 'Now I'm a woman of means.'

'A kept woman,' he says.

It was for Ruaraidh that I had come here, giving up my job in the hopes of more permanent closeness, here on the island of his birth.

'Who's keeping me?' I asked.

His dog-teeth shone brightly as he laughed.

'*Uill, m' eadalt,*' he said. '*Chan eil ag obair.*'

Chan eil ag obair. It doesn't work. Which meant, where others had, inside them, a calling, a vocation, I had nothing. The thought hit me solidly, a blow to the low rib, where, if I were a man, God would have made Ruaraidh out of me. I was not a translator, but that word *eadar-thangair* pressed itself into my thoughts. I couldn't help but think of this *being between tongues* as the same as *being between jobs.* A place of loss, of purposeless. Or a place where purpose is yet to be found.

I went to take a shower and get ready for class. Pyjamas off, the water hot, eyes averted from the mirror before that summary glance, a quick-as-you-dare checklist of the places I hid from myself with clothes. I had one foot in the bathtub, ready to pull the shower curtain between me and my reflection, when I stopped. I stared. A hole in the side of my abdomen, the length of a fifty-pence piece on its side. And when I pulled back the skin to peer in deeper, there was nothing. No appendix, no inflammation or herniated knots. Nothing. That's what was inside me: nothing.

If I had seen organs, the liver-sheen, or a marbling of fat, maybe I'd have gone to the doctor. Maybe I'd have told him about the rain, and this feeling I had, whenever I came up against Gaelic, that something was changing. But when I pulled the wound to look inside... How to describe it? Not even blackness. A blank. A space without colour or dimension, without any sense of shape or texture save where the skin had crosshatched at the edges. This is how I think of skin now: as material. It can be cut and sewn and reshaped, but in the end we take if off and step out of it, the way we step out of a dress after work. The same way we wear our names in Gaelic. A meaningless scrap waiting a wash, left after the soul walks out of it like a sleepwalker through an open window. Soft, muffled collisions.

The mirror steamed. I was lost to myself. Quietly, I stepped into the flow of water, and felt it touch that space inside me where something wasn't, where something might be, where something lay waiting.

*

How do I fix it? How do I fix it? That has always been my question. When my parents divorced, I said: How do I fix it? When my boyfriend didn't like the movie I picked when I was sixteen, I thought: How do I fix it? And there, too, as I sat and stared at a space, an opening, blushing, almost tentative – the perfumed edge of a lily – all I thought was: How do I fix it?

I should have left for class ten minutes ago. Ruaraidh was at work. He had work. I didn't. *Chan eil ag obair.* Though we met through work, in another life, when I had a job. I gave it up to come here, for him, to be with him. To make good on a promise. To make good on a dream. I should have left for class but I knew, somehow, that I wouldn't find there, in the Bengal rain and the colours by rote, what I was looking for.

The hole didn't hurt. In this wound there was no pain, but shame, and an intense knowledge. The kind you have one day when the heart finally gives way. The kind the consumptive has, when the fist comes away with blood. It meant an ending. To what, I couldn't say. The hole spoke simply, gravely, of finality.

I packed my Gaelic dictionary and decided to walk into the land, into the names of things. I wanted reality, objects, things I could touch and feel. I looked up the names of things: mountain, river, peat. *Monadh, abhainn, mòine.* I wrote them down, in the back of my notebook, great expansions of words along an empty column. An invisible spine and the vocabulary lungs, a living organ. I thought I felt, under my fingers, breath in those pages. There was parity, there, between the English and the Gaelic. A balancing of the equation. If only things were truly that simple.

I settled down on a rock – *air creag* – and looked out, back across to the island, toward the stones of Callanish, hidden behind their vale of ash-grey stone. Callanish. A circle and a meaning that is lost. *Calanais, Callanish.* The two words faced each other in my dictionary as if on opposite sides of a mirror: here the Gaelic, here the bastard Scotticism. When I looked up the name Carrie, all I found was *giùlainte, carried*, and *adhbhar-sgaoilidh galair, a carrier of a disease*.

No balance. No scale. No equilibrium. I felt myself falling without moving. A strange vertigo in which my lungs, my heart, and some deeper piece, collapsed into the blank at my side.

How do I fix it, how do I fix it?

I thought, if I could find the names of things, then I could make better sense of the world around me. As I looked at the landscape, the slit in my rib ached with wanting. I wanted parity: between the world and the word. But there was only a gap, a fissure, a rent. And there I stood, with my notebook and my hope, in the dead eye of it. There I stood, between.

*

I heard Ruaraidh's heartbeat against the drum of his ear from across the kitchen table. An amplification. A steady signal: dot, dot, dash, dash. The blood speaks. The tongue moves air, forms words, gives voice, but the heart speaks its own language. Vibrations on the surface of dermis and membrane. A firefly pulsing against the paper lantern of its prison. It could burst out. Or be torn out. Would this be freedom?

A strange urge rose in my throat, my teeth itched. I wanted to tear Ruaraidh to pieces. I wanted to ingest him, chew him, drink even the juices, the marrow, the saliva glands, pituitary, gallstones, all of it all of it all of it all of it. The knife and fork in my hands trembled, silver clattering as I put it down on the plate, eggs untouched, and made my excuses to leave. I told him I had to get to class, though I hadn't been back since I first ventured out into the land-scape. I let the door swing shut behind me and headed out on my own course, far from the textbook.

What I wanted wasn't language, though it might have

started out that way: to be closer to Ruaraidh, to integrate, to be part of a history that is, supposedly, my own.

I stood on the street and breathed, assessed. That was before. How false it felt, now, how paltry. It was not what I wanted now. But what did I want? I was thirsty, so thirsty. And though I'd had water upon water that morning, pints and pints of it in the kitchen before Ruaraidh had even woke, nothing seemed to slake it. I wanted something. I wanted something as simple as water and though I didn't know what it was exactly, I felt, in the ache at my side, a sort of direction. The faint tremble like the kind you get in the bones of birds: a compass in the body that says, *follow, here, further.*

I found myself at the coast. The Atlantic, great grave-water, the grim dark churning. I went as close as I could into the sea, my jeans up to my knees and the waves hitting, intolerably cold, the flesh resisting as I moved further. And I knew, with each step, that I was meant to be there.

I leaned over, cupped my hands, and brought to my lips – with all the devotion of an acolyte, an anchoress, some holy fanatic – the bitter draught of the sea. I drank. And I drank. And only then did I feel the flesh of my tongue swell once more. A return of life. My very own resurrection. I felt another change, too: when I lifted up my shirt the hole in my side was the size of a letterbox mouth.

How do I fix it?

I tried to fill it with sand but it spilled down without entering, forced back somehow by whatever it was inside, some force, some energy. I tried to put my hand in and my fingers bent around the nothing inside. I picked up the sand again, but looking down at my side, I knew, I knew. Pointless. So I did the only thing I could think to do: I put a handful in my mouth and swallowed the clotted mass of it. Grit trailed from the tip of my tongue down the length of my oesophagus. But it heartened me, gave me the strength, the silt and sift. Enough to turn back to the land.

Ashore once more, I walked out past the dunes and into the grassland, before dropping down to my knees and scooping the solid earth into my mouth. I chewed it, the rocks – *na creagan* – the mud – *an t-eabar* – the roots – *na freumhaichean*.

I grabbed greedy fistfuls of dirt. I shoved my hands into the soil and prayed for my fingers to grow, to tangle, to become one with the roots of the earth, its breath, the tides that are its pulse. I ate the land and its names and the nameless sea. And only then did my hunger, slightly, so slightly, abate.

How do I fix it? I no longer knew what I wanted to fix: the hole in my side; myself, maybe; or simply this terrible wanting that only lessened when I drank the sea and ate the land and took its names inside me.

But I knew, there, sand on my legs and mud in my fingernails, that that kind of hunger can never be done. It eats and eats and leaves you starving. I looked up to the sky, ravenous. If I could have reached out and touched them, I would have eaten the stars, the moon, the sun. I wanted the heart of things. I wanted their essence. I wanted to bite into it, drink it, the very marrow of the world. Instead I stayed there, on my knees, wanting and wanting and wanting.

*

I laid my clothes out on the bed, considered them. What to take? What to wear? Now that I had done it, severed ties.

The house shook as the door slammed shut. Ruaraidh had left, after our talk. When I told him that I was leaving this place, where I had dreamt of floured surfaces and hand-kneaded bread and knowing the neighbours and the air of the house thick as soil with the feeling of home. And instead I had only come to know that I didn't belong there.

'Where, then?' he asked.

'I don't know,' I said.

'Is it someone else?'

'No,' I said. 'It's me.'

The bones of the house settled, after the shock of Ruaraidh's parting. The island outside the bedroom window lay still. The Western Isles were once called the *Innse Gall*, the islands of strangers. A reference to the Norsemen who occupied and raided the shores. In the place names, they say, the coast is in Norse, but the heart of the isles is Gaelic. But there is something under the heart. Something ungraspable. A hole that the earth and the sea cannot fill.

I got up to open the window, breathed in the night air, and began to undress.

On the bed, among the clothes, was my notebook. As though, when I ran out of clothes, I might put on the words and wear them instead. On the page I could make out: *Dubhradan* (m). *Sable.* The colour of the night sky. Beside it I had written: *blind man's buff.* A search in the dark. That wasn't the page I kept going back to, though. I found myself stuck where I'd written the word for translator: *eadar-thangair.* Someone who lives between tongues.

I can't travel between two tongues. I come up short. I find things transforming in the wrong direction. There is a gap, a slippage, a space where the words do not fit. I find myself yearning not for Gaelic or for Norse but for the names the rivers call themselves and the sweet secrets of the earth. But water has no language and the soil has no words. These things are as foreign to them as the Norsemen to the *aibhnichean. An Innse Gall. The Islands of the Strangers.* Everywhere there are strangers, foreigners, things unrecognisable. Only sometimes, with time, do we learn to love them. And then, like the tide, what we love becomes strange to us once more. But what is it that makes us forget how strange we are to ourselves?

The wind came in through the window, lifted the air, spoke, as if expecting a response.

I spoke, there, alone in that room. To myself or to the wind. I said the words I'd learned: *Balbhanachd, balgaich, coibhair, cobhar, frith-bhacach, smid, smior-chailleach, smod, smodan, smolamas, taisbeanach, taisealan, tannas, uileadh, uipear, uipinn, urracag, urrag, urrain. Urralachd. Gorm.*

The words lay on one side of the spine in my notebook, their English equivalents on the other. I hadn't quite managed to sew them together. Their breath was out of sync. *Barbed, thole pin, child, author, impudence, appearance, breaking, blue.* But the words themselves were a rhythm, a voice. Every one of them changed me. Even now, when I say the word *gorm* a Bengal rain starts to fall in my head. I throw my head back and drink it, the fresh water as it drips from gulmohar leaves, the thick palm, along my tongue and down into whatever it is that lives there, under the skin, under the voice, pressing itself like music against the taut skein of the heart.

Out of the window, there was a sky without rain. It seemed to me that, at a certain frequency, or a certain intensity, I might be part of it. The marrow of things. I just had to peel back language, words, names. If I could do that, I thought, then I could do anything. All things can unravel, here, on the edge of things. There is danger in a life between tongues – but a promise, also.

The wind tugged at the bare opening at my side. Unbearable. I wanted it to be over. I wanted it to be done. And there, on the edge of things, I gave in. I yielded. It was so easy. All I had to do was stop asking myself how I was meant to fix it. There was never anything to fix. And when I felt that, when I felt it truly, down deep in the depths of me, something came away, freely, and settled among the other garments on the bed. Discarded. For a moment I couldn't remember it ever having belonged to me, though for all my years of life, I had worn it.

When it started, when it all started, I thought: how much less I was, how deficient. Seeing things and hearing things and thinking things I shouldn't. The more I learned, the less I felt. Each gain came always with a loss. But maybe it's OK to lose a part of yourself. It makes a space for something else. Or maybe I was never losing anything: maybe I was simply expanding a possibility.

I left there, on the bed, as if sleeping: my old life, my notebook, my name, my skin.

I stepped out of the window and into a dream.

Eilean nan Sgamhain
(The Isle of the Lung)

The cusp of his chin on the red of her bobble hat, resting; a kiss, rolled clumsy by the pitch of the sea. Daniel watches the two of them from a seat outside the ferry's observation deck, how the strength of the wind from the sea unsettles the pair. A rearrangement, a shuffle of down jackets and mittens, then they are once more stable: young lovers perched against the rail of the ferry prow. Daniel watches them take in the Atlantic – hematite, savage – as the styrofoam coffee cup cools in his hands. He retreats into the stout wool of his overcoat, tries to remember what that felt like – warmth, bodies unafraid of the elements, those small touches, the easing shifts, how the man's hands wrap around the woman's waist, how he draws her close to his chest. But the memory is so far away; not just space but time. As though with each mile the ship puts between them and the dock in Oban, Daniel's memories grow further still. As though he cannot carry them with him, this far northward, past the most outer of the Outer Hebrides, to the institute on Eilean nan Sgamhain. A thrilling thought. And, at the same time, terrifying.

'How do you pronounce "An Sgamhan", anyway?' the woman asks, her hands wrapped around the man's, rubbing them absently, her gaze focused on the rag wash of ocean.

'Don't ask me,' he replies. The accent is northern – Aberdeen, maybe. Daniel imagines the apple-shaped chamber in his throat, the vibration of voice in tendon.

'You're Scottish, you're meant to know.'

'Not all Scottish people speak Gaelic,' he says. 'It's not like Ireland or Wales. It's a dead language.'

Daniel turns away, tries to focus on the plash of waves. There is something in what the boy has said, the magnitude. That so much should be irretrievable.

He looks into his coffee. Thin, institutional. He had looked into one not dissimilar, in the hospital, while a priest had tried to console him, the last rites performed, at the insistence of Aidan's mother.

Take strength in the resurrection.

'Hello,' a voice says.

He turns to address it, and finds himself staring at a man in his middle years, who has sat next to him on the bench outside the ferry cabin. Daniel raises an eyebrow at the black robes the man is wearing: vaguely religious, but without denomination. His head is shaved on the sides, the grey on top sleeked back in a small knot, wrapped around itself in triplicate.

'Hello,' Daniel replies, shifting in his seat, ready to escape.

'First time on An Sgamhan?'

There is a note of practice in the man's pronunciation: the 'mh' said as 'v', the first 'a' a leap into air.

'What makes you say that?'

'You have the look,' the man replies, casting a rueful look at the couple. 'Do you know what it means?'

'An Sgamhan? The lung, no? That's what the brochure said.'

The man nods. 'In a way. An Sgamhan. The Lung. But it is more than that, more significant than that.'

'Go on,' Daniel says. 'What's your sales pitch? Hare Krishna? Buddha? Or is this something else you're peddling?'

The man snorts. 'Peddling? I'm just making conversation. The trip to the isle is long, and gets boring without' – he looks at the young people, considering – 'company.'

'Well if it's that kind of company you're looking for, I'm not interested,' he says.

The man shakes his head. 'So ready to cut the connection before it's made. But then again, that is the way with you people. Is the isle the first time you've ever heard the word *sgamhan*?'

'Yes,' he says, not sure how else to respond, trying to work out how to get out of the conversation.

'Do you know Loch Scaven?' the man asks. 'It's near Glen Carron.'

'East of Applecross, right? I drove by it once. A road trip with—'

He stumbles. Aidan.

'That's the one,' the man says, taking up where Daniel has trailed off, unfazed. 'Loch Sgamhain, in Gaelic. The lake of the lung, or the loch, if you prefer. They say a kelpie used to live in the loch. Ate travellers, as kelpies do. Do you know how they knew? Because it would always leave one thing behind: the lungs.'

'Why are you telling me this?'

'You have the look,' he said, tilting his head. 'You seem open.'

'To what?'

'Why do you think the kelpie refused to eat the lungs?'

'Fussy eater?'

'Because it knew: the lungs are sacred. *Pneuma*, to the Greeks. *Anima, animus*. Breath and soul. Like Anaximenes tells us: "Just as our soul, being air, holds us together, so do breath and air encompass the whole world."'

'What's that supposed to mean?'

'Just something to think about when you're on the island,' the man says, clapping his hands on his knees as he stands up and stretches. 'It should be coming into view about now, though it'll be a while before we can dock properly. Treacherous currents. You should go up to the railing and see it. It's quite a sight, the first time. And if you'd like to hear more, come find us, on the isle.'

He leaves before Daniel can ask him who 'us' is, his robes at odds with the pristine quality of the deck's plastic and metal finishes. Daniel shakes his head. Is there something about him, now, he wonders, that attracts this? Grief some quality of the air?

He walks up to the rail, slowly, taking his time at the bin on deck to separate the recyclable parts of the coffee cup, reminding himself that going up to look is in no way obeying. He lays his arms on the rail and looks out, over the waves, as a scrap of black grows large on the horizon. An island out here, erected in this space beyond the farthest stacks and islets, here where no island had ever been before. New land for a new world. Or so they said.

The brochure had described the process: how the seabed had been raised, the land shaped, trees planted, genetics accelerated, so that in the space of a few months they towered, taller still than the oldest of the primeval redwoods. A huge arboretum in the shape of a lung, housing the research of the An Sgamhan Institute. An educational resort, and the gem of Scotland's booming new trade in ecotourism.

Aidan would have loved it.

The island lurches closer with each breath. The swell of wave seems somehow in tune with this movement. Maybe it is simply what the man said – maybe he is too open to suggestion, now – but each surge seems to join, somehow. The flow of wind, the rhythm of his breath. He has the sense of lifting, of being part of something larger, as Eilean nan Sgamhain approaches.

Maybe Dr Murray had been right. Maybe this trip would do him a world of good. He breathes it in, this sense of promise, the roll of sea and air, and watches it grow closer. Eilean nan Sgamhain. The Isle of the Lung.

The hotel room is modest, alpine, variations on wood: a sauna, a hot tub, a flat-screen television, wall-mounted, floor-length windows along the other. The thread count on the sheets is staggeringly high; their white a shade seen only in commercials. He cannot bring himself to touch them – something about their expense, a pleasure in things not yet touched. Instead, he sits in a mock Eames chair, grey leather, his laptop open on the table in front of him, the trees through the window reflected on the darkened screen.

He should be going out there, into An Sgamhan proper. That had been the idea: to drop his things off at the hotel, on his way out. But there is still the hesitancy, the fear. Eilean nan Sgamhain has not changed that, despite what Dr Murray had said.

He goes to the coffee maker, stuffs the oversized sachet into the centre, fills the plastic tank from the bathroom tap, and puts a video on to wait for it to brew. After a coffee, he tells himself, he will go out, get dinner somewhere in the An Sgamhan resort, where already he can hear families going out for early dinner, children laughing, shouting, screaming. The brim and boil of life.

Two cups of coffee later, and she is still on his laptop screen in her magenta powersuit, shoulder-padded, her eighties hair speckled under the grain of the original VHS recording. It would have been possible, the man at the shop had told him, to clarify the image, for an additional fee, but he had declined the offer, preferring instead the feel of authenticity the tape gives the scene. As though the past itself is congealed there. A singular moment preserved.

'In the Western lowlands, we can expect to see a wave of low pressure coming in from the Atlantic, bringing with it heavy rains and strong gales,' the woman on screen says. His mother.

Strange how something as slight as weather should seem so important since Aidan died. There is something almost arcane in it. Six o'clock news. BBC Weather. Oracles of frost and precipitate inclemency.

It's because she's dead, he thinks.

Nine years prior he had buried her, Aidan by his side. The metal of their wedding rings pressing tight as he gripped his hand and laid her body in the earth. She had borne no resemblance to the woman on the screen by then. With each second the body becomes a stranger to itself, it seems. It is only in the tape that the moment can be held. Tapes he had discovered only recently, going through Aidan's things. A box of his mother's thrown in the attic, so he could rush into forgetting, telling himself, one day, he would have the strength to face them. As if the items were too charged with an energy only time could lessen.

Dr Murray had told him not to bring them, to leave his laptop, if he could, and if not, to be certain to remove the videos from the computer. An external hard drive. A dispelling. But how could he?

He looks at the room, its pristineness, the unruffled bedspread. And he knows he cannot bring himself to touch it because it is a double bed. Meant for two.

'And in the Western Isles, things are looking a little drier, with rain coming in overnight and lasting till morning.'

He spreads the photos out, in front of the screen: holiday photos in Budapest, Instamatic memories of his cousin's wedding on Lewis. So many angles of approach, different locations, different lighting, and still some part of Aidan escapes the lens. His hands rest on the photos. The light between the trees lessens as his mother talks to him, from 1982, about weather patterns long past.

A rain begins to fall outside. He takes it as a sign, orders room service, and brews another pot of coffee – he had long ago given up on sleep – before leafing through a brochure of the An Sgamhan Institute while his dead mother talks pressure fronts.

The island itself, despite the claims, is only vaguely shaped like a lung: a lazy sort of crescent, with the institute covering its entirety. The dockside resort is the size of a middling mall, and contains hotels and restaurants, shops, and a cinema to keep the visitors entertained when the main attractions close for the night. He follows the path with a finger, up through dense forest, to the nucleus of the island, which is the An Sgamhan Institute itself, and attached to it, the great auk sanctuary. Both open to the public, the brochure tells him; educational tours in reforestation and genetic recovery.

All the elements on Eilean nan Sgamhain were as they should have been, in the plan, the one they had been putting together for so long, putting off until they both had time, thinking, with the self-assuredness of the living, that tomorrow was promised.

Aidan would have loved it.

A sharp rain against the windows. He looks up to the percussion. A ghost-image, there. He finds himself waving at it, slowly, the movements inverted, in the glass. For a moment, it seems to be someone else. But then the image returns, and it is just himself, the photos, the video, disappearing in the patter on the window and a sentiment blurred by rain.

Tomorrow. Tomorrow, he tells himself. He will go out, into the trees, on a tour of the island, among the great redwoods, leatherwoods, the pine; things planted here, the brochure tells him, to counteract the ills of the century, merchant capitalism, and industrialisation. He will not stay inside, in the mouldering dark. He will not ache for what is lost. His mother in the earth nine years and Aidan in his grave only a few months now. He will not taste ash with every bite, will not find his fingers searching for fingers no longer capable of giving them warmth. He will not struggle to breathe in a world filled with air. Tomorrow, he tells himself. Tomorrow. As he goes over to his suitcase and takes out more photos, while on the screen, his mother speaks meteors. Her words coming from some place outside the world. Some place still capable of sustaining them.

The bird waddles through the forest path. Its black and white form reminds him of a rudimentary penguin, and if he had to describe it, he would probably say: unlovely.

The great auk, *gearra-bhall*. A seabird last seen in Scotland at Stac an Armin in 1830, before the species became extinct after the last two birds and their egg were killed for museum display in 1844. Stac an Armin is part of the archipelago of St Kilda, the guide explains, in the west of the Outer Hebrides, and where in 1930, after two millennia of habitation, the last of the residents were evacuated after their way of life became unsustainable. Now Hiort is an important breeding ground for birds, she says. She uses the Gaelic name for St Kilda; Hiort, the word said like *hursht*. Daniel listens to her pronunciation, to check the sounds, see if she really knows what she is talking about, not knowing himself what the Gaelic should sound like, relying instead on some sense of it in his imagination.

A dead language.

Whoever named the great auk must have had a sense of humour, he thinks. It is far from great, but it is amazing, nonetheless, that they should be able to reproduce, here – with a few stray genetics – a bird unseen for nearly two centuries. While the islands it had once called home – Hiorta – remain lifeless, inhabited only by conservationists and tourists.

The guide explains to the meagre group – Americans, mainly, a Chinese couple and a Filipino gentleman, cameras and phones, their clicks insectile – as they tread the path that winds its way from the edge of the cliff, that when the last natives of St Kilda departed, they left on their tables an open bible and a pile of oats. To nourish what came behind.

'Shouldn't it be possible,' Daniel asks, raising his hand to interrupt, 'to do this sort of thing with humans? The auk, I mean, not the trees.'

'In theory,' she says, eyeing the rest of the group as if

147

expecting an ambush. 'But the moral implications prevent it from being applicable.'

'What do you mean?'

'What would be the point of living,' she says, 'if we could always be brought back? And what if the dead didn't want to live again? Would we just kill them? We don't practise husbandry on humans, sir – that would be eugenics. We haven't stopped death. We've simply found a way to bring back what went missing.'

He nods, dissatisfied, then wanders off from the group as soon as he can.

The auks, for their part, seem quite happy with their island out of time. He sits on a rock while they mill around each other, mindlessly content. He should be overwhelmed by this display, but all he can think of is the image of a bible and a pile of oats, left behind to nourish – what?

One of the auks comes away from a group of its fellows to stare at him. He remembers what Dr Murray had said to him: to let himself feel, to allow the connection. He holds his hand out to the auk, fingers trembling, as though the bird were connected to some larger idea. Will it bite? But then, Dr Murray had said, we always risk pain. When we choose to love; to live our lives in the open air.

The bird considers the hand, waves its stubby wings as a sign. Looking at it, Daniel wonders if it remembers its past life. If memories are stored in the genes, or whether the bird had been born blank into this new millennium. If they brought Aidan back, would he remember him? Or would it be a stranger with his face?

Daniel shivers, nauseated. Those eyes he had seen into, looking back at him without recognition. The thought of it.

The auk squawks, then wanders off, into a world never

meant for it, and a world it was never meant for. His hand stretches after it, calling it back.

Why doesn't it understand? That they are the same species. That without Aidan, he, too, is out of place. Living this way, remembering, walking the path they had laid in front of them, thinking, one day, they would walk here together. The last of his kind. It's stupid, so stupid, to feel even lonelier now, without the bird.

But he had hoped. For a moment. He had thought, here, at least, on this island outside time, he might be able to breathe easy again. In its scouring wind, tinged with salt, which lifts his tears as it passes. Daniel puts his hand under his coat to remove the chill. But no hand reaches into the grave. What is lost remains lost.

The video plays. A tropical storm in Cuba. A meteor shower in Iceland. He watches the Orionids scratch light in the aurora. His mother speaks over, explaining, before the camera shows her once more in the studio, peach suit and lemon blouse, make-up too heavy for how young she was then, how young she is, projected this way.

Would it be possible to reconstitute her from this? Plot the trajectory age would take her, the features which he had grown used to, as she neared the end? Or does it require a speck of saliva, a skin flake, dandruff? Are these things more us, in the end? Is this all we are – a genome, stem cells, code?

Why then should he feel, watching her, that what the tape captures – the moment, the expression – that these things are her? That the image is all she is?

In the darkened light of the hotel room, where Aidan should have been, sprawled on the bed with a book in his hands, talking to him about climate change, responsibility, how much we owe each other: love and justice, a liveable world. The kind of passion that had made Daniel fall in love with him, a passion that seemed so much larger, more expansive, than how he lived – a habit of being, what Aidan had called, in his exasperation, 'perpetually distanced'.

But not with Aidan. Never with Aidan.

He has no video of Aidan. Photographs, yes, though too few, too static, failing to capture the ease of movement, the way his right eye flickered when he was riled, the way he smiled when exhausted. Of this, there is no record. Only memory. Memories which fail in their resurrection, and grow dimmer each day, though ache no less to touch.

An accident, on Loch Lomond; a friend's boat at the weekend for poker night, and a last-minute trip to one of the islands in the middle of the loch.

If he could, he would. Go back, record every waking moment, commit the curve of scapula and clavicle, the tilt of hip and thigh, to records, blueprints, and schemata. But what would it be, without its animation, the electric charge of mind, the inner propulsion which causes the chest to rise and fall? He does not believe, like Aidan's mother, in the economy of the soul. But there is something, still, something.

Dr Murray had told him he had to come to terms with his loss. But he isn't quite sure what it is he has lost. And he cannot locate it, in the images, the fragments, or the render of tape. What is it that is missing? What is it that cannot be brought back?

This is what being dead must be like, he thinks, forcing himself to continue on through the mist that has come in overnight. An Sgamhan half there, in *harr*, the tall pines vanishing beyond their first spare towers. A world half formed. Things fallen back into creation.

The An Sgamhan Institute rears from the mist, circular buildings attached, like bracket fungi, around a glass dome at the centre. The heart of An Sgamhan.

In the queue for entry, to the front of the institute, where the opaque glass is at once a rebuttal and an invitation, there is a small booth and screen in which – for a small fee – it is possible to have a photo taken, though the image is displayed for everyone to see as they wait in line. The camera is a kind of atomic X-ray, where oxygen, nitrogen and carbon dioxide are visualised as strands of light pouring in and out of the body. The composition of the threading is changed with each breath. By the time he is near to entering the institute itself, he recognises the couple moving toward the booth.

To his surprise, once inside, they kiss. The camera records their held breath, the movement of oxygen into the nostrils, how the lung fills, the way their bodies press. The camera captures their composition; even their bones seem familiar to him.

'Sir?'

He shuffles forward and pays his fee, embarrassed by his inability to turn away. Something in the moment had spoken to him. Something like an answer.

The interior is ethereal; the air has the feeling of spring. The exhibit consists of small rooms where trees are cultivated in nurseries climate-controlled for time period and genus. The nursery rooms upstairs are connected to a larger space in the centre, where the young trees grow fuller, their growth controlled by the peculiar process of acceleration for which An Sgamhan is known. Walkways through air, the same opaque glass as the walls, transparent railings. Walking them, he feels at once supported, and at constant risk of falling.

He stands and looks out over the trees, some already beginning to exhibit that strange power that draws the eye upward, others still shrub-high, barely out of their nursery cells. In front of one or two are some figures in familiar black robes, kneeling, heads bowed before the trees.

'They think they can attune themselves to the cycle of the trees,' a voice says. Daniel looks to his side to see a man standing there, arms crossed, leaning over the glass partition with no fear. His face is younger than the grey that runs through one half of his beard and up the side of his head, where the curly hair has been shaved in on the sides, but still topples messy on top. Daniel feels a sharp spike of desire, then the slow wash of shame.

'What?' he says, already feeling the heat in his cheeks.

'The people in the robes. Our very own cult. It's quite charming, really. Like a fan club.'

'You, uh, work here?'

The man laughs. 'Yes, I'm in charge of the nursery project. These are my babies.' He gestures to the trees lined up in a row in front of them; the figures prostrate in front of them.

'It's wonderful,' Daniel says. 'The way you bring things back. Things that people thought were lost.'

He wrinkles his face. 'You sound like that lot,' he says. 'Nothing's being brought back here. The trees are trees, we grow them, the birds in the sanctuary, new birds from some old genes.'

'But the whole point of An Sgamhan is restoration, isn't it? Restoring the ravages of the environment.'

'That's one way of looking at it. Personally, I think we're in the business of recovery.'

'What's the difference?'

The man shrugs. 'The point isn't to restore what was lost. We're healing what is. The organism, the world, it won't survive at the rate it's going. We aren't salvaging some remote past. We're preparing the world to face the future.'

There is an echo in what he says. He sounds like Aidan.

'And you think it'll work? You think the world is ready to face the future?'

'Ready or not, the future's coming. We do what we can. I'm Matt, by the way.'

They shake hands, the grip a little longer than necessary.

'If you want to learn more, you could always have dinner with me tonight.'

'I…' he begins. 'I can't, it's not that I don't want to, it's just…'

'You don't have to explain. Life just gets a bit remote on the island; eligible bachelors my age don't normally come through. You can't blame a man for trying.'

They stay there, looking.

'I met one of them on the ferry,' Daniel says, gesturing to the people in robes around the trees. 'Talked to me about some Greek philosopher. Lungs and breath.'

'They do that,' Matt says.

'What is it that brings them here, exactly?'

'They think there's something here,' he says. 'The way the process is condensed. A sacred spark in the atmosphere or something. Beyond that, I don't really pay attention. Anyway, I really should be getting back…'

Images. A book, a table, a pile of oats. A hand held out to something long dead, but living still. The cold. The loneliness. The lungs in his chest. With great effort, Daniel reaches his hand out again, grabs on to the sleeve of the medical coat, as if pleading for remedy.

'Stay?' The word spills out his throat. 'With me... For a minute. Just... Stay?'

Matt looks at Daniel's hand for a moment, considering, then looks him in the eye. He nods, comes to stand by him on the railing, and nothing more. Their arms press against each other. Something stirs in the heat of it. Daniel looks out over the trees, and feels, there, something new. He breathes in, desperately; trying to capture in his frail hand, in some crevice of alveolus, whatever it is in the air. Whatever it is that makes him feel, for the first time in so long, alive again.

The Atlantic seems more temperate, this time round; still its slate tumult, but without the fierceness he felt of the approach. It seems like an old friend, now, as the ferry leaves An Sgamhan – hydrogen motor almost silent, the peel of the horn announcing his return. Home. To his memories. And whatever is left.

He places a hand to his chest, feels the oblong in the inside pocket. A single photo. He and Aidan, outside a tent, on the trip to Applecross. The rest are packed away, the files on the computer archived. Whatever it is he is looking for in them, he knows it is not there, now.

Next to the photo, innocuous, almost, is a business card: Matthew Bromer. PhD.

He starts at a sound, familiar but yet not, and stares at a young couple, wrapped in each other, near the prow. They are not the same as the one he came with; but they move the same, hold each other the same way as they talk. The wind lifts the words, somehow jubilant, the Gaelic at once strange and alive. The meaning is beyond him, but the words are music. The sweep of the vowels tangling in air.

For a moment, an image flashes in his mind: a pile of oats, scattered on a table like seeds; an open book, the wind flipping pages, searching for something in the sentences. Taking a deep breath, it seems that, with just a little effort, he might be able to reach out and touch it. And he is no longer afraid – to try, at least. To reach out. To whatever it is in the air; whatever is left. Something that still speaks, faint as breath, from its place outside the world.

Acknowledgements

'A Gift of Tongues' was first published in *Cōnfingō* in 2018. It was included in *Best of British Fantasy 2018* (NewCon Publishing) edited by Jared Shurin and *Best of British Short Stories 2019* (Salt) edited by Nicholas Royle. 'An Inheritance' was first published in *PANK* in 2015. 'This Impossible Flesh' was originally performed and commissioned for LGBT History Month Scotland in 2013. 'Les Archives du Cœur' was first published on *The White Review* website in 2015. 'In Ribbons' was first published in *The Masters Review* in 2015. It also won the 2015 Masters Review Short Story Award.